TRACKS

PRAISE FOR TRACKS

"...White-hot passion and unrelenting suspense will keep readers of *Tracks* on the edge of their chairs. In this superb romantic suspense novel, author Libby McKinmer skillfully weaves a tale of bravery, love, and psychotic treachery. Readers will cheer gutsy police detective Emily Evans as she hunts down a serial rapist terrorizing the women of Yorktown. They'll fall in love with the tough, heroic newspaper editor, Mac Landon; and shiver with revulsion at the demented actions of the psychotic villain, Jack Martin...McKinmer's smooth writing technique provides a seamless, fast-paced read, perfectly in sync with the tension-filled plot. Her vividly-drawn characters carry the story line with style and distinction. *Tracks* is highly recommended to all who crave a novel they can't put down until they've read the very last word."

—J. L. Abbott
Author of *The Third Corner*
and *The Bluecoat Affair*

"...A suspenseful and exciting tale that moves fast and furious to its thrilling finish. The interaction of Emily and Mac is sensual and steamy. The author's portrayal of the rapist is chilling and his evil is a tangible force. He is a very believable villain. Fans of suspense won't be disappointed by this book."

—Brenda Gill
Timeless Tales Reviews

Also By Libby McKinmer

Betrayed By Love

TRACKS

BY

LIBBY MCKINMER

Libby McKinmer

AMBER QUILL PRESS, LLC

http://www.amberquill.com

TRACKS
AN AMBER QUILL PRESS BOOK

Amber Quill Press, LLC
P.O. Box 50251
Bellevue, Washington 98015

ISBN 1-59279-997-3

Rating: PG-13

Layout and Formatting provided by: ElementalAlchemy.com

PUBLISHED IN THE UNITED STATES OF AMERICA

Dedication

To Doug...always

Prologue

The sun sank behind the skyline as he stalked into his shadowy den. The furniture had become only indistinct shapes, but that didn't slow his progress. Not for a moment. He saw well in the gloom and he'd allow nothing to affect his movement.

What he headed toward summoned irresistibly from its hiding place. His inner tumult grew as he closed in on it.

The secret cache.

It was a tribute to his exploits; a shrine to his intent. Right now, he needed to touch it, see it, rifle through it and feel it in his hands.

Tonight, he brought a new offering to his hallowed collection. This fact sent joy coursing through him, enhancing his pleasure in the evening's upcoming strategy planning.

His smile brimmed with anticipation. It emanated from a place deep within, a place always exhorting him to pursue new trophies.

Adrenaline glutted his veins, his pulse escalated. Next to the actual conquest, this was the part of the chase he savored most. The game had begun, but his quarry sat as innocently oblivious as a deer in an autumn clearing unaware of the hunter's high-powered rifle sighted on her from his blind.

After arriving at the ornate antique desk, he pulled open the second drawer and pushed a tiny groove on the edge of the desk. With an ominous click, a concealed niche popped open. He reached in. The only item in the hiding place was a small album with dozens of pages. The hunger increased as he sank into a chair and turned on a single light in the darkening room.

Before he made his addition, he allowed himself to review past triumphs. His nerves hummed as he thumbed through already-full pages. Most displayed pictures, some included personal items like hair or fingernails. All of them had one thing in common—each page contained a small newspaper ad. His excitement hit a fever pitch as he pulled the newest ad from his pocket.

He stared at it for a long moment, acknowledging it as a symbol of the new direction his hunt was about to take. With it, he'd altered his process, and that change thrilled him. For today, instead of responding to others' personals, he'd placed *his own ad* in the paper.

This ad.

The small piece of newsprint looked fragile in his long-fingered, strong hands as he flipped to an empty page in the album and carefully peeled back its protective film. He centered the ad in its place of honor at the top of the page, leaving room for mementos of the upcoming pursuit. He smoothed back the plastic, licked his full lips greedily and shifted restlessly in the chair. Soon she would respond, writing and begging him to single her out from the many who wanted his special attention.

His unknown prey's spoor was strong and her trail crystal clear to him. He could barely wait to begin. But he tamped down his excitement knowing his tactics had to be mapped out with cunning. His quarry would be wary and skittish, which made the game even more challenging for him. An easy victory was never his aim; he was exhilarated by his victim's efforts to escape him, especially once she realized the game had begun in earnest.

The more she struggled to escape her destiny, the more he enjoyed the contest.

Tonight, he was eager and primed to step onto her trail. He just had to wait for her to respond to his ad. He'd identify her as soon as he read her letter. Then, the hunt could begin.

One more time.

CHAPTER 1

Emily sighed heavily as the division lieutenant signaled to her across the noisy precinct room. Her desk overflowed with files needing her attention. Somehow, she didn't think he was about to help her clear it off.

Most files she was working on involved paperwork. She admitted to herself it had been thoughtful of her colleagues to make the first weeks of her return after the hiatus a bit easier. After all, recovering from a gunshot wound wasn't child's play. But she was getting bored with parking ticket follow-up and presenting crime-proofing demonstrations to service clubs.

The lieutenant beckoned to her again. Emily jumped to her feet, pasting on a smile.

She decided he had something more on his mind than another lunch meeting—he always left the assignments for those little gems sticky-noted to her desk lamp while she was at lunch or on break. She jogged to the waiting officer, noticing at the last minute he held a stack of files in his hands.

Oh, no, not more paperwork.

Emily stopped in front of the grey-haired veteran. "Hey, lieutenant, you got some work for me?"

Her sultry, sexy voice didn't match her no-nonsense approach to life. Still, it had proven useful. It was her just-out-of-bed tone that had established her reputation on the phone sex sting organized by Yorkton Police the year before. But it also led some men to assume she was less intense, intelligent and committed to criminal justice than she was.

If that was a man's first blunder, it was the only mistake she allowed. Emily didn't give second chances to men who saw her long legs, trim body and wavy, shoulder-length auburn hair as her main attributes and best traits. She didn't make a production out of dismissing men who only saw the physical. It was nothing more than a fact of life and that's how she treated it. They weren't worth her time.

"Yeah, Emily," Lieutenant Axworthy said. "I've got some files here I need you to look at."

"Sure thing. Can they wait 'til this afternoon, sir? I've got the mayor's wife's parking ticket coming up in court this morning. I'm supposed to be there if I can."

"I'd rather you send the information over with Rodriguez. These files need your attention right away. Frankly, I don't think anybody else can work on this the way you can, Evans." Emily didn't miss the tension or the sense of urgency in Axworthy's voice.

"Okay, sir, what've you got for me?"

"I know this might be tough for you to listen to, but I want you to hear me through." He looked down at the stack of files he was holding. "Come on into my office." He led the way to his tiny cubicle and shut the door behind the young detective.

"Is this something new?" Emily was confused. Why hadn't her commander just dropped the files onto the stack already accumulating on her desk?

"Well, yes and no. The cases span the last few years. For a while, we didn't suspect there was a connection among them. I mean, cases like these are so tough on the victims and their families, sometimes they aren't even reported."

Suddenly, Emily knew what her lieutenant was leading up to and why he wanted her to listen to all he had to say. She swallowed hard, forcing herself to remain silent although the urge to object was almost irresistible.

"Sometimes women don't want to report this kind of a crime and I can't say I blame them. Lord knows, I've always thought the tests to collect physical evidence were difficult enough for the victim to handle. And even during the smoothest investigation, the case can take on a life of its own." He paused. "I'm not telling you anything you don't already know, am I?"

"This is a sexual assault case, isn't it, sir?" By now Emily's heart was pounding madly in her chest.

She remembered too well flying to New Orleans to identify her sister's body in the cold, stainless steel morgue of the downtown police station. She recalled the bruises in sullen relief against the stark white of Rowena's naked body. No place on her sister's slim body had been immune to her attacker's brutal rampage.

"It is, Emily. I'm forming a task force and I want you to be at its head."

"No, sir, I can't." The words were out before Emily even consciously thought them. "I just can't go there again."

"Emily," his voice was kind but firm. "I'm not making this an option. I need a woman officer's perspective on this case. You are our most experienced female detective. And," he reached across the desk and touched her hand gently, "I believe you can relate to these women in a way that'll give them a sense of control again. They'll see that no matter how frightening and difficult this situation is, there's a place on the other side of the experience where they're safe again."

"Safe?" Emily's voice rose. "Rowena was never safe again, was she, sir? I couldn't save her, could I?" Her shoulders slumped as she stared into Axworthy's compassionate face. "I can't offer these women anything at all," she ended in a whisper.

"That's where you're wrong, Emily. I think you have a great deal to offer. Something Wilson and Thompson and Shaw can't."

Emily raised tear-filled eyes to him.

* * *

Axworthy steeled his heart and continued. "I want a female officer involved. The only other woman detective in the division available to work this detail is Angela O'Connell. You know she just passed her exam last spring, Emily. She's not ready to take the lead on something like this."

"And I am?"

"I think you are. I think this is exactly the right case for you." Axworthy smiled at her. "It'll get you back into active duty. And with you in charge of this investigation, I think this rapist might as well turn in his personal possessions to the booking sergeant right now."

* * *

"I don't know—" Emily started to say. Then she looked up at her lieutenant, the man who had made the arrangements to bring home her sister from New Orleans, the man who had studied with her for her detective's exam. The man her father had called friend for half a lifetime. What she saw in the sad, blue eyes was belief in her.

And then, Emily believed, too.

He picked up the top file and handed it to her. Emily took it as gingerly as if it were contaminated.

"Use my office. I've got to rattle some chains out there in the squad room anyway. Wilson's on his third coffee. Time for him to hit the streets." The lieutenant stood up and walked to the door , then turned back to face her. "This will never bring back Rowena and I know that. But you *can* stop what's happening in Yorkton."

Emily nodded and looked at the stack of files on the desk. There were at least eight of them and she dreaded opening even the first file cover. But she pushed down her pain, flipped open the folder and began to read. By the time she was halfway through the first record of rape, she had grabbed the notepad on the desk and was making memos to herself.

Lunch came and went. Emily wolfed down an egg salad sandwich as she pored over the chronicles of the predator stalking the streets of Yorkton.

By mid-afternoon, she had completed her review of the files, and had compiled a stack of notes and lots of questions. Even though the investigating officers on the various cases had done a good job of gathering information, Emily knew she was going to have to re-interview some of the victims. Because she now agreed with Lieutenant Axworthy. There had to be only one man involved in every assault. She felt it. Even with only one shred of DNA and no fingerprints or even a decent description by any of the victims, she felt a chilling thread running through the cases.

The attacks were too organized to be random. The women involved didn't know one another except in the most peripheral way. They were all well-educated, each had a good job and they lived in safe neighborhoods. Two had married since their attacks and the other six were still single. Each had visited the sexual assault crisis center, Oasis, and had talked to a different counselor. Each woman had gone to the sexual assault treatment center and had had the attack evidence gathered by nurse practitioners. Each had informed the police of her assault and wanted her attacker caught.

The police had no suspects.

"I know you're out there," Emily murmured. She looked at her notes. Her smile didn't reach her heart. "And you're not going to hurt anyone else."

She would need to talk to each woman who had been attacked.

Emily dreaded that task—for them and for herself. She had no wish to dredge up pain and anger each had undoubtedly worked hard to overcome.

But she felt the aggressor's presence in every case. She might have only a scrap of evidence, but she knew he was there. His malevolence was almost tangible to her.

And the worst of it was, she felt he was searching again.

Predators like this one didn't stop. While eight of his attacks had been reported, other victims probably existed—women who had not spoken of the incident to anyone.

Emily consulted her notes. She was sure from the addresses on file that one of the molested young women lived in her own neighborhood, an area with plenty of lighting, regular security patrols, well-maintained homes and an established neighborhood watch network.

She found what she'd been searching for in the section about Joanna Halton. The young woman had been sexually assaulted in her garage after returning home from work the previous September. She dialed Joanna's home phone number listed on the inside jacket of the file.

"Hello. Thanks for calling. I'm feeding my attack dog, so leave a message and we'll call back later." A tone followed.

"Hello, Ms. Halton. My name is Detective Emily Evans and I'm working on a series of sexual assaults in the area. At your convenience, I'd like to meet with you to talk about your case. I live just two blocks from you, so if you'd feel more comfortable talking to me in your own home, I can easily drop over one night after work. Assuming the evening would be more convenient for you, of course. Please call me back." Emily left her home and work numbers and hung up.

What were the chances Joanna Halton would call back, she wondered. Maybe Joanna wanted to forget she'd ever been assaulted.

Emily looked through the folders again. She wrote down the names and phone numbers of several more victims, picked up the phone and dialed the number for Karen Addison.

"Hello?"

"Hello, is this Ms. Addison?"

"Yes. Who is this?" The voice was suspicious.

"My name is Emily Evans and I'm a detective with the Yorkton police."

"What can I do for you, Detective Evans?"

Emily could hear no encouragement in the woman's voice. "I'm leading an investigation into some sexual assaults in Yorkton –"

"I can't help you." The rushed words cut across Emily's sentence. "I don't want to come to the station and talk about it all over again. I don't have to."

"Ms. Addison, of course you don't have to come to the station. I'd be happy to meet with you wherever you'd be comfortable."

"Comfortable? Talking about what happened to me?" Sarcasm dripped from each word.

"Ms. Addison, it would really help with the investigation if—"

"I did my part last year when I reported this. The police told me to go to the hospital and have evidence collected. Which I did. I filed a report, obtained counseling and have gotten on with my life. I have no intention of returning to that time."

"Ms. Addis—"

"Thank you for calling, Detective Evans, but don't contact me again."

The click in Emily's ear was definite.

During the next hour, she reached two answering machines and a disconnected number. Even her attempt to track down the owner of the disconnect was fruitless.

Emily glanced at her watch. Her shift was almost over. She had to find a replacement for tomorrow's Elks Club lunch meeting. There must be someone else who could teach the club members how to burglar-proof their homes. In the meantime, she needed more officers on her task force.

As she strode back to her desk, files in her arms, she scanned the detective room. Angela O'Connell was hard at work at the desk beside Emily's. While she might not have been a detective for long, Angela had been a beat cop for five years and had a lot of one-on-one street experience with people. Emily stopped at her own desk and set down the armload of files before she headed over to the chair at Angela's desk and dropped into it.

"How's it going, Em?" Angela's short hair was standing up on end and she tried, unsuccessfully, to smooth it back into place. "I must look a mess," she apologized, "but you know how paper work makes me pull my hair out."

"No problem, Angie. I've got a proposal for you, but there is some paper work involved."

"Why can't we just dictate our reports into a voice-recognition computer? That way we can avoid the paper and stay out there catching the bad guys."

"I feel the same way."

They both understood paperwork was necessary, and that it was every cop's cross to bear. Each criminal activity generated a mound of it. Emily suspected that an investigation like the one she was about to launch with her task force, would create a mountain range. She also knew the task force's files would have to be maintained meticulously. In fact, too many criminals walked free because case work had been shoddy. A defense attorney loved nothing better than a cop who cut corners on the files.

"What's up, Emily? Something I can help with?"

"I think so. Lieutenant Axworthy has given me some sexual assault files to review. He's thinking about putting together a task force to work on them. If you're interested, I'd like to ask him to include you. What do you think?"

"Tell me more." Angela shoved the file she'd been working on to one side.

"A number of young, professional women have been sexually assaulted in Yorkton over the past couple of years."

"Nothing unusual about that, unfortunately," said Angela.

Emily nodded, thinking about how many times rape investigations led police to someone the victim knew—estranged husbands, co-workers, boyfriends, even dates.

"I sense there's something different about these particular cases." Emily paused and looked directly at Angela. "I think there may be a serial rapist in Yorkton."

Angela sucked her breath in through her teeth. "A serial rapist? Here?"

"I think so, but it's going to take legwork—and paperwork—to find the guy. Are you interested?"

"In putting a sicko in the slammer? You bet." Angela slapped the top of her desk. "It would mean a lot to me. A friend of mine—you remember Jen who came to lunch with us last month? She's a nursing supervisor at Yorkton General Hospital. She was raped last Tuesday night after her shift. We've got no clues, not even a complete description. She said he never spoke and he wore a surgical mask, scrubs, latex gloves and a condom. Her file may not have made it to Axworthy's desk yet, but I bet she's a candidate for your theory of a serial rapist."

"Any leads we can work on?" Emily could feel adrenaline begin to pump. The surface details were similar to every case sitting on her desk. "Is she married or did she have an ex-boyfriend or a jealous lover?"

"She's divorced, but that happened years ago. Steve lives in Denver and has remarried. She's not dating anyone right now and her last boyfriend is a really great guy. I know him personally. My husband and I even double-dated with them a couple of times. He's an optometrist or something. Even so, I talked to him about it and he has an alibi for the time of her assault. So, yeah, if I can help find a rapist, count me in."

"Let me talk to Axworthy and clear it, but I absolutely want you on the team, Angela."

* * *

By the next morning, the team was in place and ready to begin re-interviewing the women who had reported assaults over the past few years. Emily had assigned Angela to review the details of Jen's attack with her friend. She'd also provided Angela with a list of questions, the answers to which would provide a concrete connection between Jen's assault and the rest of Emily's cases.

After hours of poring through the files, Emily found a connection among several of the cases. At least three of the women had told investigators they'd met their ex-boyfriends through personal ads in the *Yorkton Daily Gazette.*

Emily had a place to start.

Within minutes, she divided the eight files between two task force members, Angela and Ryan James, a detective with eight years' experience. "This is a long shot, but find out who met her last boyfriend through the personals," she urged them. "Ask them what he did for a living and get a physical description of each boyfriend."

There had to be a clue linking all these crimes, whether it was the boyfriend's eye color, workplace, hobbies, or his build. Maybe the personals ads bound together the cases.

Emily was eager to begin and she marched into her lieutenant's officer with alacrity. "Hey, boss. What's up?"

"Emily, good morning. Not much, except I hear you've commandeered a couple of my cops to fill out your task force." He grinned at her. "Good choices."

"Thanks. I know you said Angela lacks experience, but I think her five years on the street qualifies her to join me. She knows how to talk to people, get them to open up to her."

"I said she didn't have the experience to *run* the task force. She'll be great on the team. " He hesitated for only a moment. "Ryan James is a good man to fill out the squad, but remember, he's still getting over his partner's murder last year."

"I know. But that makes him vulnerable. I think some of these women will pick up on that, perhaps see him as accessible to them because of it. Plus, I've never seen anybody go through evidence and pick up clues like James. He's the one"—she looked mischievously at Axworthy— "who really taught me how to read forensics and showed how they can apply as evidence in court."

"And not me?" Axworthy was mock hurt. "Seriously, Ryan James is the best I've ever seen. I'd urge him to become a forensic criminologist, except he's also a great detective and I'd rather have him in my department." He laughed. "James rounds out your team perfectly."

"I've got him breaking down the cases for evidence even as we speak, although there's precious little to analyze. Every one of the women was assaulted in a place where she felt safe—either her home, her office or her car. Each reports the same scenario.

"Her assailant was completely covered. Sometimes he wore a ski mask, sometimes a surgical mask, once he even had on a breathing mask…you know, Lieutenant, the kind you wear when you're working with chemicals or insulation? It makes you look like a bug. No one ever saw his face, so we don't have a physical description other than average height and weight with an average build.

"They all reported he wore latex gloves and a condom. He never removed his pants. This guy planned to leave no DNA behind. In fact, we found only one sample. A single strand of hair. It's all we've got, and we've nothing to compare it to at this stage of the game."

Emily looked down at her notes quickly. "While each victim had her hands taped together from wrist to fingertip—probably so she couldn't scratch him—only two had their mouths taped shut. In the case of three others, he tied a scarf around their faces during the attack. With each of the rest, he put a ski mask over her head to prevent her biting him. He seems to have thought everything through very carefully."

Axworthy nodded. "But there is a link. I can feel it, can't you?"

"Definitely. I think the same guy has attacked each one of these women. The M.O. is too precise to be more than one person. I don't think his choices are random either. Also, I think this guy is a predator. He feeds on the whole choosing and stalking of his victims."

Axworthy stood up and held out his hand. "Well, Detective Evans, he made a fatal mistake when he started hunting in your city during your watch. The hunter is about to become the hunted."

"And the captured," Emily stated grimly. "I don't care what it takes. This guy has come to the end of the line."

* * *

As midnight approached, he pulled his last letter off the laser printer in his den, a small smile on his face. He'd written responses to the women who'd answered his ad. Among this select group, was his next prey.

Tonight his snares would be laid and he would begin to bait his trap.

He could feel the gratifying pounding of his blood and the surging in his groin as he left his den. Through the twilight, he walked a few blocks, opened the mailbox and deposited his letters.

"Soon, my sweetling, soon."

Blood throbbed brightly as his voice caressed the threat.

CHAPTER 2

He was running late this morning, but the time he'd spent searching through the myriad of responses to his ad was worth the inconvenience. So many women, each entreating him to select her as his new consort. His excitement had surged to the apex of his control at times, and his body had flooded with yet-unreleased hormones.

Just as in the past, he could get to know his target and compel her to trust him implicitly. She'd become emotionally involved with him before he staged their breakup. Then he'd employ his hunter's conquest of her unwilling body and soul.

With one last regretful look at the captivating letters and photos still piled on his desk for his consideration, he carefully locked his den door. He grabbed a coffee and began his short trek to work at the newspaper office.

*   *   *

At mid-morning, he paused to check his traps. A glut of envelopes crammed the mail box assigned to his assumed name. His excitement grew as he contemplated how different this hunt was from the others. He'd never before set up himself as the bait. Would there be a flood of young women, each begging to become part of his world? Each inviting him into her personal territory? It appeared so considering the volume of mail already waiting for him in Box 24M47. Triumph thrummed through him. So many responses, and today was only the second day after his ad had appeared in the personals column.

His hands ached to grab a handful of the envelopes. He could barely wait to sift through this crop of them. Choosing a new target was always so satisfying, so energizing. His every stalking sense was heightened now that he was into hunting mode.

Glancing around the teeming newspaper office, he acknowledged that he couldn't afford to have anyone suspect him. Too many people milled around him to risk seizing any of the envelopes now. He practically groaned his frustration aloud.

But when his work for the day was done, when the office was empty, he's use his key to come back and retrieve the cache of letters. In the haven of nightfall, he'd take them to the shelter of his den. There, surrounded by his bygone trophies as tacit witnesses to this search, he could pore through the multitude of desperate pleadings for his special brand of personal attention. In privacy, he could peek into the dreams of his quarry and choose the one most suited to his tastes, the one who would become his next tribute sacrificed on the shrine of his hunting lust.

He knew he'd never bother with the people whose ads he had answered. It was much more satisfying to watch his trophy choices parade in front of his watchful stare. If this new process worked well, from now on his pursuits would be much easier. He could just advertise for a new quarry every time the urge struck.

He shivered with anticipation.

As he turned away, he saw the secretary for the advertising department stuff two more envelopes into his mail box. He moaned softly to himself as he returned to his desk, bearing a cup of coffee for the woman at the desk next to his. With a smile, he handed her the coffee and went back to work.

* * *

Emily started her work day with a phone call she'd been thinking about making since the night before.

"Good morning, Yorkton Daily Gazette."

"Hello, I'd like to know the name of the managing editor, please."

"That's Mac Landon. May I connect you?"

"No, I think I'll stop by and see him in person."

"Well, Mr. Landon is running somewhat late this morning and won't be in until after eight-thirty. You might have better luck calling back later to schedule an appointment."

"Thanks very much." As Emily hung up, she reflected on how little she knew about Mac Landon. Time to learn more about this man.

Emily was smiling slightly when she arrived at the newspaper offices shortly after eight-thirty. For some reason, she could hardly wait to meet Landon. Was it because he could be her link to the man she sought? She pushed open the glass door and headed toward the receptionist behind her highly-reflective stainless work station. As Emily strode across a vast open area interspersed with potted trees, she noted the modern, tasteful décor.

"Could you tell me where the managing editor's office is, please?" Emily asked the friendly young woman.

"Yes, ma'am. Mr. Landon's office is on the same floor as the advertising department. You just go down the hall there." She pointed to her left. "Make a right at the first corridor and you'll see a bank of elevators. If you take the express to the twenty-third floor, you'll find the advertising department. Mr. Landon's assistant can help you from there. Her desk is just to the left when you get off the elevator."

"Thanks." Emily couldn't help grinning to herself as she followed the directions. Now she was being addressed as "ma'am." She probably wasn't any more than eight years older than the receptionist.

Oh well. It's better than the quaint Southern tradition of referring to women of a certain age as "old miss."

Emily easily found the elevators, and in a few short moments of silent ascent, arrived at the twenty-third floor. The doors glided open and the young detective collided with a flurry of activity rivaling that of her own detective division office. Men and women rushed about, most with papers in their hands and a harried look on their faces. Everywhere phones rang and computer printers sloughed out endless reams of paper seized by employees on their way across the office. She paused a moment to get her bearings.

"Can I help you, miss?"

Emily looked around for the source of the disembodied female voice.

"Over here, dear." A grey-haired woman on the near edge of the tide of activity waved enthusiastically to catch Emily's attention.

"Sorry," Emily apologized, "I was a bit overwhelmed for a moment." She grinned and the woman returned the smile.

"That's no problem. I keep saying they should move my desk right outside the elevator, but Mac says he couldn't keep himself organized without me at his office door. I keep the onslaught at bay." The grey-haired woman fluttered her hand at the chaos around them. "But he doesn't fool me. Mac is the most organized manager I've ever worked for. He knows exactly what everybody should be doing and if they're doing it." She paused to take a breath and scrutinized Emily. "Did you want to place an ad, dear?"

"Well, no, not really," Emily was still off balance from the secretary's zealous greeting. "That is, I'd like to see Mac Landon if I could."

"Hhhmmm," his secretary acknowledged as she flipped through an appointment book on her desk. "He's pretty busy from ten-thirty on, but I'm sure he can see you before that."

"Great."

"Actually, he's usually in by now, but he's running just a little bit behind this morning," she confessed chattily. "That's not like him, but I guess we're all going to be late every now and again. Why don't you grab a chair over there and I'll give you a yell when he's in and settled."

Another vigorous signal pointed Emily in the right direction. The young detective murmured her thanks and took a chair where she'd been pointed. After pulling out notes from her shoulder bag, she started reviewing them. Fifteen minutes later, the elevator doors slid open and a man stepped out.

He caught Emily's notice immediately. He paused and glanced around the room. Apparently satisfied with what he saw, he headed toward the secretary's desk, nodding pleasantly at Emily as he passed her. She smiled back. *This has to be Mac Landon.*

Emily couldn't help but be impressed by the man. He was about six feet tall and extremely handsome. His square jaw was clean-shaven. Trendy, wire-rimmed glasses framed brown eyes. Dark, slightly wavy hair was casually ruffled and he ran his hand through it in an attempt to slick it down. It worked only partially.

Dressed in a navy Tommy Hilfiger suit and carrying a leather briefcase, Mac Landon looked like he'd just walked out of an ad in *GQ* magazine. He was definitely what Emily and her friends referred to as a "hunk." And he was in perfect condition. His wide shoulders, accented by the padding in the suit jacket, tapered to a slim waist and hips. His long legs carried him easily across the room at a rapid pace Emily knew she'd have trouble matching.

He stopped at the grey-haired secretary's desk and talked to her quietly. The woman handed him a few slips of paper then pointed to Emily and spoke animatedly to him. He said a few more words, turned and smiled at Emily, then went into his office. The secretary gestured her over.

"Well, dear, he said he has to return some urgent phone calls, but then he can see you for a few minutes. That is, if you don't mind waiting just a little longer."

"No, I don't mind," Emily said as she mentally reviewed his physical appearance. It fit the description of the rapist exactly. He also shared other characteristics with their profile. He was organized and obviously personable.

"Can I offer you a coffee?"

"Sure."

"I'll take you by the staff kitchen on my way over to the typesetting room, but if you don't mind fixing your own, I'd sure appreciate it."

"No problem at all. I'll even fix you a cup, if you'd like."

"You are indeed one of heaven's angels, young lady," the woman bubbled as she made her way across the tumultuous office. "I take mine black."

In the kitchen, Emily took her time searching for styrofoam cups, milk and sugar. As she worked, an attractive man in his mid-thirties dashed into the kitchen and grabbed the carafe she'd just set down.

"Some mornings are just two-cup mornings," he exclaimed as he refilled his travel mug and raced out of the room before Emily could do anything more than raise her eyebrows.

She wandered back to the waiting area, dropping off the second coffee on the secretary's desk. By the time she'd only half-finished her own cup, Mac came out of his office.

He walked over to her and stretched out his hand. "Hello, my name is Mac Landon. How may I help you?" His voice was deep but soft. This was not a man who controlled his staff through ranting and raving.

"Emily Evans." She stood up and shook his hand. "If you have a few moments, I'd like to talk to you about the personals."

"Well, there's not much to say, Ms. Evans. You can place an ad for a day, a week, a month. Whatever length of time you'd like. So it's less confusing, we have a glossary defining the terminology." He grinned, and took her breath away as she watched his smile light up his dark eyes. "So don't worry if S-W-F doesn't immediately translate to single white female in your head. We can provide the jargon for you.

"The cost of your ad also includes a mail box that we issue here at the newspaper office. Your ad identifies that box number only, never your name, and all responses are directed to that mail box so your identity and your privacy are protected. You can drop in and check on replies anytime Monday through Friday during regular business hours.

As far as cost goes, it depends how many words are in your ad and how long you want to run it."

"Well, your description is quite thorough!"

" I'll set you up with an ad rep, but I must warn you, Ms. Evans. This is not the safest way to meet new people. There're a lot of individuals out there"—he gestured to the world at large—"who are not above lying, or shall I say obscuring the truth about themselves. Are you really sure you want to place an ad?"

"Actually, I want to talk to you about your department's procedure." She flipped open her purse and pulled out her badge. "I'm directing a task force looking into a series of rapes in Yorkton. My investigation has led me to your advertising department."

Mac's handsome features froze. His brown eyes iced over. "Why didn't you identify yourself earlier?"

"Would it've made any difference? Right now, all I want is to ask a few questions about how the personals work."

"Well, no," he conceded coldly, "I guess it wouldn't have made any difference at all. Procedure is procedure. It's a matter of public record for anyone who wants to place an ad."

A frigid, dismissive expression was etched on his face as he started to turn away. Clearly, he'd decided they were finished. Emily touched his arm to stop him. He jumped as if she'd scorched him.

"Okay, I can appreciate that." Her husky voice deepened slightly as she looked up at Mac's still frosty expression. "But do you have a few minutes so we could discuss this investigation further in the privacy of your office?"

* * *

He was surprised at her request. He had expected his cool withdrawal to signal to her that the interview was over. He hadn't foreseen she'd want to discuss anything more with someone so obviously rankled by her presence.

He gazed at her with sudden curiosity. Most people fled when he froze them out with his cool, crisp words and glare. Yet, this unruffled young woman merely returned his appraisal with an expectant expression. His mood and his obvious dismissal seemed to have made absolutely no impression on her.

"Mr. Landon, all I need is a few minutes. This is a very serious matter."

Recovering himself, he nodded, "Of course. Come into my office. It'll be a bit more quiet in there." He stepped aside and motioned for her to precede him into the room.

*   *   *

Emily was amazed by Mac's office, but she didn't betray it. For some reason, she'd expected an ultra modern space with metal and sharp edges. Instead, she felt like she'd stepped back in time. Rather than typical vertical blinds in an institutional neutral, the windows were covered by roman shades. Two area rugs in warm colors spread across the floor. A massive oak desk in one corner dominated the room; there were books everywhere. A green-shaded banker's lamp provided plenty of light in his work area and an upholstered chair had been shoved back from the desk. This part of the office exuded a lived-in feeling.

Mac indicated a leather couch against the wall behind the door. In front of it sat an antique coffee table covered with more books and magazines. Hanging above it was an English hunt scene. Lamps on the end tables offered soft, clear lighting. Emily noticed the overhead fluorescent lights were off and raised window shades allowed natural light to flood the work and reading areas. The remainder of the office was more muted. All in all, the room was soothing, especially when contrasted with the pandemonium in the main office.

Emily sank onto the couch and smiled up at Mac who'd remained standing. "Are you going to sit down?"

"Yes, of course," he replied. He sat down beside her. "I'm sorry, what did you want to talk to me about?"

"I need to know a bit more about staff interaction with advertisers." She knew she'd have to handle this part of the questioning very carefully to avoid spooking him or tipping her hand.

It was not going to be easy. Especially when his every glance, angry or not, registered so strongly with her. As she set down her coffee cup, she slanted a look at his profile. Mac Landon was a very handsome man, she decided. But part of it was because he seemed inured to his own good looks. They were such a part of him she somehow knew he had forgotten what he looked like and his possible effect on women. He'd moved beyond acknowledging his appearance a long time ago.

Her eyes were inexorably drawn to his lips. Emily had never been a fan of full lips, but Mac's were just ample enough to make her wonder how warm and firm they'd feel against her mouth. She thought they would probably move gently against hers at first, testing her interest. She began to feel her own instinctive response. Her lips parted and her tongue moved in answer to her thoughts, touching the bottom edges of her front teeth in anticipation of his tongue's arrival at the entrance to her mouth. It would be warm and probing, she knew. Emily could almost feel the dance as their tongues grazed, touching and teasing, escalating their ballet of sensation.

His lips, now damp-hot from their hungry melding, would move away slightly, prolonging the passion leaping between them before he swept down on her mouth again, devouring her spiraling ardor with a fervor of his own. His tongue, dueling with hers, would carry them toward another plane of pleasure as his hands joined in his exploration of her.

She glanced down at Mac's hands, resting casually on his knees. She could almost feel his long, strong fingers trace a path down her cheek and along her jaw-line. Delicately, his hand trailed to her waiting breast. His index finger circled Emily's expectant nipple under its scant silk covering. It rose to meet his touch eagerly, peaking in anticipation of a more intimate caress.

Mac avidly obliged her body's needs, unbuttoning her blouse as he momentarily pulled back from his enjoyment of her mouth. Gazing into her eyes, he tugged open her blouse and dropped his stare to her firm, high-set breasts. He slid the blouse down her shoulders and his hands drifted back up her arms, stroking her. Emily could easily see his reaction to his exploration of her body.

She knew his hands would be firm, but warm and gentle on her body. She welcomed Mac's caress of her willing skin and dropped her head back against the soft leather of the couch thrusting her bosom high for his enjoyment.

He accepted her invitation but, before voraciously pressing his mouth to her aroused flesh, Mac captured Emily's breasts tenderly between his hands, closed his eyes and skimmed his face appreciatively over their soft firmness, teasing her turgid nipples even higher. His tongue flickered over her heated skin and she murmured incoherently as desire ruled her every motion. Desperate to feel Mac suckle at her, she stayed his exploring mouth at her swollen, darkened aureole.

She felt his lips open against her and suddenly the seductive wetness of his tongue sliding over her nudged Emily's longing to a higher plane. Gently his teeth closed on her sensitive skin and he flicked her captured nipple with his hot tongue. She was stunned by desire. She had to feel his skin against hers. Greedily, she pulled at the buttons on his shirt hearing them pop and skitter across the floor as they gave way under her anxious fingers.

She feasted her eyes on the revealed wide expanse of muscular chest. Dark hair formed a dense thicket and she slid her hands into the curls as she took his nipple into her mouth and brushed it gently with her tongue, teasing him as he'd tormented her with mouth and hands. He groaned aloud. But she needed more. She had to feel his skin and the crisp chest hair against her. She shrugged out of the blouse still drooping off her shoulders and urged him to his feet with her. Leaning into him, she smoothed her naked upper body against his, pressing her breasts into the firmness of his chest.

She shimmied gently against him, pleasuring them both with the sensation of silk on denim as her soft skin was gently abraded by his chest hair. She craved more. Stepping back, she ran her hands over his chest again as she gazed into his eyes, a slow smile on her kiss-dampened lips. Looking down, she reveled in the sizable swelling straining toward her through the soft wool of his trousers. She smiled openly at him. He was feeling the same passion as she was. Her lips parted seductively and she let her fingers wander across him at will, whispering for him to touch her, too.

In silence, they took their time, touching, caressing and arousing one another. She felt his sharp intake of breath when she allowed her hands to follow the dark vee of hair down his muscular stomach and under his belt. She looked up at him as her fingers unbuckled the belt and unbuttoned the top of his pants. She saw his arousal bulge even larger as she reached for the zipper.

"I said, may I offer you a second cup of coffee?"

Emily looked up, realizing this must not be the first time he had spoken. She blushed as she realized where her musings had taken her. She was in Mac Landon's office as the lead detective of a task force, not as some moonstruck teenager daydreaming about a great-looking guy. She forced the wayward thoughts to the back of her mind and gave herself a moment to collect her thoughts by accepting his offer of another cup of coffee.

While Mac was out of the room, she pulled out her notes. By the time he returned, Emily was a composed and collected detective once more. She put the coffee cup on the table and flipped through her notebook to a blank page.

Looking up, she discovered he was watching her in curiosity. Had he read her earlier thoughts? Rattled by his scrutiny, she jumped into her questioning immediately.

"Which employees in the advertising department would know the identity of customers placing personal ads?" she began. "Would they meet customers in person, or via the phone?"

"Well, to start, we staff seven sales reps. Five of them are generally on the road, selling advertising space to businesses and companies locally and regionally. This keeps them pretty busy since they're responsible for filling all the open ad spots throughout the paper. And that's about fifty percent of every page. I'd tend to think they have minimal contact with people who place personals."

"Why do you think that?" Emily had totally recovered her equilibrium.

"Most personals are placed by phone. A few arrive in the mail, and I'd say only the occasional advertiser places an ad in person."

"What about the other two reps? Would they have direct contact with the people who phone in?"

"Yes, they would. Jack has worked in classifieds for about four years and Amanda has been here, I'd say, twelve years. Both are good employees with solid customer service skills. Is there a problem with one of the newspaper's employees?"

Emily shrugged. She wasn't ready to show her whole hand just yet. "Are they the only two who'd have information about those who place personal ads?" She felt as if she had to dig every detail out of him.

"Well—" he paused, obviously thinking about her question. "Anybody in the department could look at the daily mockups on any computer terminal in the section. And, I suppose, it wouldn't be impossible to figure out which mailbox goes with which advertiser if you really wanted to know." He looked directly at her. "But anybody, and I mean anybody in the department, could figure it out."

"Even you?"

CHAPTER 3

"Even me." He held her scrutiny steadily, without so much as a blink of his dark eyes. He nodded toward the computer on his desk. "Given enough time, I'm sure names could be matched up with ads placed without too much problem."

"I don't mean to press you, but there's a man systematically stalking and raping women in this city. It's my job to figure out who he is and stop him, Mr. Landon."

Her husky voice unwittingly caressed his name and he felt jolted by his immediate reaction to such an everyday familiarity. This police detective was definitely not like Sipowicz in NYPD Blues. No, indeed. This particular detective made him think about what she'd look like in and out of her dress blues. He couldn't stop his mind from following that thought and his seasoned imagination almost made him groan out loud at his certainty of how she'd look.

At just that moment, she uncrossed her long, athletic legs and leaned forward to pick up her cup of coffee. He forced himself to concentrate on why she was seated beside him on the leather couch in his office.

"What makes you think someone here at the paper is involved?" He disciplined his mind to focus on the task at hand instead of her legs.

Her next words startled him back to the cold reality of why this captivating detective was sitting beside him in his office. She wasn't here to flirt or drink coffee. She was on a deadly serious mission.

"My investigation has led me here."

* * *

Emily paused for a moment and considered her options. If she was going to tell Mac what was going on, she'd have to be sure he wasn't a suspect. She'd discovered nothing of the predator in his attitude. He did not appear to be hiding anything. He'd been cool and precise in his answers, but had not attempted to evade any of her questions. Emily let her gut decide.

She looked the editor straight in the eye. "As I mentioned earlier, there've been a number of unsolved sexual assaults against women in Yorkton. These attacks have a few unusual things in common."

Mac gasped as the significance of her words appeared to sink in. "A serial rapist in Yorkton?"

She continued, "The other members of my task force and I have recently reviewed the files of a number of women who reported being raped. All of them fit a similar profile. They're independent women, professionals mostly, in their late twenties to mid-thirties. None of them has any history of abusive relationships and most were recently involved with decent men."

Emily filled him in on other similarities of the assaults. She finished, "We believe this man carefully chose these women and stalked them before raping them."

"But I still don't see what this has to do with my newspaper."

"The only other thing these women have in common is that all of them found their last boyfriend through the personals in this paper. Or so it appears at this point."

* * *

"Oh, my God," Mac whispered in horror. "He's targeting women through this paper?" As the realization hit home, he jumped to his feet and began to pace the room in agitation. "What can we do?" He stopped cold, ice running through his veins as he looked at Emily. "I know exactly what I can do. I can shut down the personals as of today." Mac strode toward the door.

Emily stood up and quickly moved to intercept him. Only inches from his lean, athletic body, she raised her face and stared deeply into his eyes. For some reason, he felt he had just passed a very important test.

"If you do that, he'll know someone is on to him. I don't want that."

"But what if he strikes again?"

"That's just what I'm counting on," she retorted as she took Mac by the arm and led him back to the sofa. She tugged him down on the soft leather beside her. "I want him to go on the hunt one more time."

Mac looked at her in horror. "Did I hear you accurately, Detective Evans? You want this man to attack another woman in Yorkton?"

"You heard me absolutely correctly. I want this predator to think he's undetected. That his crimes have gone unnoticed. I don't want him to know anyone has discovered the link among his targets. I want him to search out a new quarry." She paused and looked at him. "And I need the help of your newspaper to do so."

"I can't believe—"

"Wait for just a few seconds and hear me out, please. I don't want to put anyone else in danger, so this has to be just between us." She reached up and placed her palm against his chest. "I need your help if I'm going to catch this twisted stalker before he assaults another innocent woman."

He looked down into the determined face. Along with tenacity, he saw a deep sorrow in her eyes.

"You're determined, but I also sense sadness around you. Would this have anything to do with your resolve to catch this monster?" he asked kindly.

She nodded mutely and sank back onto the sofa, staring down at her hands clasped white-knuckled in her lap. "My sister died at the hands of a rapist in New Orleans."

Mac sat on the edge of the coffee table and instinctively reached out to hold her linked hands.

"Rowena was on a modeling assignment. She was first brutalized, then left to die in a ditch beside a country road. No one ever found the man who did it." Emily pulled one hand free and looked up as she tucked a strand of wavy hair behind her ear. Her inhalation was wavering, but she continued. "I had to go to New Orleans to identify her body. Then we brought her home and buried her."

She looked down again, gathering her composure once more. "I will not allow a rapist to invade Yorkton and terrorize its women." She stared at him defiantly. "I need your help to stop this."

He was nodding before her request was out. "What can I do, Emily? I mean Detective Evans."

"Please, do call me Emily." She smiled at him and he felt his heart warm at her gift. "It appears you and I are going together on this. I think it's appropriate we should be on a first name basis, don't you?"

He grinned back. "Good enough, Emily. Now, how do we go about trapping this deviant?"

"*We* don't. I do."

Mac was confused, but only for a moment. Her next words transformed his confusion to anger and fear.

"It seems, Mr. Managing Editor, that I would indeed like to place an ad in the personals section of your paper. So, would you please direct me to Jack, the man who has been taking at least some of the calls from women looking to find a man through the classifieds?"

"You can't be serious?" He was incredulous.

"I'm deadly serious."

"But to set yourself up as bait? And bait for a man who could stalk you, rape you and Lord knows what else if he even suspected you were a cop? You can't do that. Let me talk to Jack if you think it might be someone here at the paper. Maybe he's noticed someone with an unusual interest in who is placing personals." His gaze was pleading. "Hell, I'll even let you question him right this minute if you have any suspicion he could be involved.

"I'll bring him in this office now and you can catch him off guard if it's him. Which I really can't believe it is. Never once has Jack even given a hint of being less than a good guy. He even volunteers to do Santa duty at the hospital's pediatric wing every Christmas."

"Mac," she interrupted him quietly, "this is my job. I'm a cop and this won't be the first sting operation I've participated in over the years." She shrugged. "I have to tell you. The first suspect I just ruled out—is you."

"Me? Somebody actually thought I could be capable of such atrocious actions?" His anger was white hot in an instant and his blazing eyes pinned her to the sofa.

* * *

"No," she reassured him, "I know you're not."

She matched his stare abjuring any anger. Hurt feelings had no place in her investigation. Finding a man who preyed on women was paramount.

"But until an hour ago, we'd never even met one another. How could I know anything about you, let alone if you were capable of such a crime?"

Something in Mac had reached deep into the frozen core of Emily's being, to the part of her that had become paralyzed when Rowena had been murdered. She recognized this man would be vital to her and she sensed Mac would become involved in more than just her investigation. That reality was as clear to her as the couch she was sitting on. And as tangible. For some reason she didn't yet fathom, it was critical to her that he understand that.

"And now?" His stare challenged her.

"And now I believe you could be my greatest ally in this battle, Mac. You're not the kind of man who'd ruthlessly attack a woman and force her to an unwanted intimacy." She stared into his dark eyes, easily delving behind his irritation to his soul where his revulsion at what he'd just learned shone clearly. "I don't see the cold, flat soul of someone acting a part. I believe you're a truly compassionate man outraged at what's been happening."

The electricity suddenly flashed between them so brightly she was sure she could see it. And in that moment, the part of her that she'd thought had died with her sister, glimmered with the spark of life.

I've been waiting for this man all my life.

She took a deep breath to calm her roiling emotions. Before she and Mac could explore the attraction that had developed so quickly and powerfully between them, they had to stop a rapist from attacking another innocent woman.

"So," he said in a business-like tone, "let's get that ad in the paper. Are you sure it has to be you?"

"Positive."

"I mean couldn't we just set up a dummy post office box and a police psychologist could analyze the replies?"

"If this guy is as smart as I'm afraid he is, he'll come across as very charming, very sensitive and very low-key. He won't leave behind clues. This man revels in the pursuit of the woman he chooses. My instinct tells me he won't be content with a relationship on paper for the length of time it takes a psychologist to figure him out.

"He will want to meet her, he may even want to court her and, I think, will want to make her trust him. My trick will be to spot him, make him trust me and believe I'm taken in by him. The department's psychologist will help me with that, but this guy needs a living, breathing target and"—she smiled up at him to try and cushion her next words—"that's my job. I intend to do it extremely well. I want this deviant to find me irresistible. Until he attempts to do something we can arrest him for, all he's done is answer an ad. And that's not illegal."

"I know, but the thought of you out there for his diseased mind to fantasize about…"

"I'm a trained police officer, expecting him to try something. I'll use a pseudonym to distance myself from this guy and my real life. I've done this before and I'm good at it. Now, let's get started. Point me toward Jack's desk, would you please?"

"I'll do you one better. I'll take you over and introduce you to him."

"No." Her voice was firm even as she smiled up at him. "I'm afraid I don't want anyone here to know there's any connection between us. Just tell me where his desk is."

Seemingly dismayed, Mac conceded and gave her directions. "Don't take any unnecessary chances," he said. His voice barely hinted at his longing to be at her side.

Emily gathered her notes and stuffed them back in her briefcase. "See ya." She definitely wanted to get to know Mac better.

"Be careful."

* * *

With Mac's words ringing in her ears, Emily approached Jack's desk. Amanda, an accommodating woman in her early forties, helped Emily compose her ad and promised it would appear in the edition the following day. With a word of thanks, Emily headed back to the bank of elevators.

She was almost there when the doors began to drift shut. Emily called out, "Hold the elevator, please."

* * *

Her molasses voice flowed over him, making him think about his den and cache of names. He looked up and she was better than his fantasy. Her auburn hair billowed over her shoulders and her smile made his pulse hammer. So did her body. She was almost as tall as he was and very athletic looking. This one could be a real challenge physically.

"Thanks." She entered the elevator cage and its doors closed on the advertising office's chaos.

"No problem," he returned, showing his even, white teeth in a practiced smile. He'd been about to exit the elevator, but now he had to know what this spectacular woman was doing so close to him. *Had she placed an ad?* His heart accelerated with the thought. He had been in the typesetting room, so maybe Amanda had taken her copy.

If this woman was looking to find a man in the personals, she'd just found him.

"Pretty crazy in there, isn't it?" He wanted to hear her voice surge around him again.

"Uhmm," she replied with a noncommital shrug.

He had to know. "Were you placing an ad, too?"

She looked over at him, startled. "Why do you ask?"

"Well..." He looked down, pretending to be embarrassed. "I was placing an ad. I know it seems strange, but my last girlfriend and I had been together so long, I don't really know any women other than her friends. And I wouldn't feel right asking out any of them."

"I can understand that."

"This is the first time I've ever done something like this," he confessed. "I hope I don't meet a bunch of really strange people."

"I didn't know men thought about it from that perspective. I figured it was just women who placed personal ads and worried about who they'd meet." She shrugged and treated him to another smile. "Who knew?"

"Who knew, indeed."

The elevator glided to a stop and the doors opened onto the busy lobby. He gestured and she stepped out ahead of him.

"Good luck," he encouraged.

"Thanks. This is very important to me. I hope to find just the right man with my ad. Here's hoping." She smiled again, held up two crossed fingers and turned away.

He watched her long, shapely legs carry her briskly across the lobby. Once she disappeared out the main doors, he spun around and jabbed repeatedly at the elevator button. He had to get back to the office and check Amanda's desk.

This chance encounter was fate. He had just found his next quarry. Forget those hordes of desperate, pitiful women pleading with empty words on paper for his attention. He wouldn't respond to one more answer to his ad.

He couldn't wait to tear it out of his scrapbook. It was nothing, now. Tomorrow, there'd be a new newspaper item in his scrapbook. It would be this woman's classified that would crown the page...the page that would ultimately detail her debasement at his hands.

Won't she be amazed when the newspaper matches her with the sensitive man she met in the elevator? The one who worried about meeting the right woman?

A rough chuckle erupted before he could contain it. He scanned the crowd instantly, but no one seemed to notice. He was so superior to these clones around him.

Hot energy throbbed through him, fueling his sudden arousal. His hunt had begun in earnest. And this test would be his finest.

The elevator doors opened and he hurried into the cage, hitting the button for the twenty-third floor.

Chapter 4

It was the end of a long day. After Emily had left the newspaper office, she'd headed to the precinct to touch base with Angela and Ryan. They were poring through the files for more leads and had accumulated a pile of notes. Emily provided them a copy of her personal ad so they'd be prepared to help her sift through replies.

Joanna Halton hadn't called her. Disappointed, the young detective headed for home.

Emily had just gotten in the door when the phone rang. She snatched the receiver, half-expecting to hear her mother's voice. Instead, a business-like woman's voice addressed her.

"Hello. Is this Detective Emily Evans from the Eighth Precinct?"

"Yes, it is. How can I help you?"

"I'm Joanna Halton. You left a message on my machine yesterday."

"I remember." Emily's pulse quickened. This woman could provide a clue to the identity of the man preying on Yorkton's women, but Emily was going to have to convince her to relive a most frightening and upsetting experience.

"You wanted to talk to me about an assault I was subject to a few months ago, is that correct?"

"Yes, Ms. Halton, I do need to talk to you about that. I know it'll be disturbing for you, but—"

"Not as troubling as doing nothing and letting that piece of trash stay on the street. I don't want what happened to me to happen to anyone else. How can I help you with this?" The woman's tone, while cautious, was also confident.

"Would you be willing to sit down with me and go over the details?"

"I did that with the counselor and the investigating officers. Isn't it all in the file?"

"Yes, the file is very complete, but I thought if we could talk face-to-face, we might come up with something others might not consider significant."

"I see. Well, I suppose that's possible. Can you come over to my home tonight around eight?"

"Of course. I'll see you then." Emily was surprised by Joanna's willingness to talk about her rape to one more police officer.

Shortly before eight, Emily changed from her lounging attire of leggings and a tunic length shirt into a pair of broken-in jeans, a cream-colored silk blouse and a menswear blazer. She loosely french-braided her hair and slicked on a coppery colored lipstick. She tucked her .22 caliber handgun into her shoulder bag, shoved the thick Halton file into a soft-sided briefcase and headed out the front door.

The two-block walk revitalized her, reminding her how great it felt to be out in the fresh air. She'd spent too much time exercising indoors on a treadmill. It was time to change her workout habits.

She sauntered slowly along the route, enjoying the sight of kids playing hide and seek in their yards and skipping across paved driveways. The neighborhood's innocent busyness reminded her of her own childhood growing up in Yorkton. She and Rowena had had lots of fun. Indeed, their childhood games had provided early lessons of life—like the rules of fair play, giving someone a second chance and letting someone give you another turn. They had learned how to co-operate, and specifically, how women could work together instead of engaging in rivalry with one another. And they'd learned how to compete in a healthy manner.

In that idyllic world, they had been as good at a game of pick-up baseball as they had been playing house.

Then, life had driven them their separate ways; Rowena to her world of high fashion runways, and eventually, the tragedy awaiting her in New Orleans; Emily to the police academy and her world of criminals and felonies.

It's a long way from leading our Barbie dolls into battle against GI Joe.

As Emily turned the corner, she spotted Joanna Halton's house immediately. Even though it was barely dusk, security lights illuminated every inch of front yard and driveway. Shrubs were clipped to eight inches or less, and the only trees were slim-trunked deciduous species near the sidewalk, far away from the front door.

The garage gaped open, its interior as bright as a July morning. Two high-power halogen lights showed a bare space except for a late model luxury car. Emily suspected that the door would never be closed to provide a hiding place for anyone, and that Joanna would only drive in and exit her vehicle if the lights were on and she could see that no one waited for her.

Joanna Halton had been raped in that garage.

Emily walked up the curving walkway and paused before the entranceway. The front door was beautiful with its leaded glass overlaid by the fancy pattern of a wrought iron outer door. Emily knew an electronic lock system securing the house could only be released by pressing a code into a computer pad inside.

She rang the doorbell and, as she did, glanced up at the security camera taking her picture. In a few moments, she heard an intercom squeak and a voice asked her to display her credentials. She willingly did so, holding them steady in front of the camera. Two deadbolts slammed their release and the inner door swung open.

A tall, slender young woman wearing a grey designer suit stood in the portal. Her expression registered fear and frustration. It was obvious to Emily that Joanna Halton resented the cumbersome security system, yet relied on it to feel safe in her own home.

Emily stuck her hand through the protective grille. "I'm Detective Emily Evans, Ms. Halton."

The woman shook her hand.

"Would you like to have a closer look at my id?"

When Joanna nodded, Emily handed her the police identification along with her driver's license. The other woman inspected them, then keyed in the code to unlock the outer door.

"I'm sure I seem incredibly suspicious. You should see what happens when the FedEx guy shows up at my office before business hours," she offered with a slight grin. "Please do come in, Detective Evans."

Joanna's house was like a display page from an interior design magazine. The large, airy rooms of the main floor were exquisitely decorated in coordinated, subtle earth tones. But Emily couldn't help noticing the alarms on every window, panic buttons in several accessible locations and a security door with another computer lock leading to the second floor. Still, the décor was so exquisite, Emily knew it was only her cop's eye that allowed her to see the safety devices so readily. To a guest, the panic buttons would be unobtrusive and the door with its discreet security lock would go unnoticed.

"Sit down, Detective Evans." Joanna indicated a chintz wing chair directly across from the couch where she was seated. "I see you've noticed my home protection equipment." Her voice was fiercely unapologetic.

Emily nodded.

"I had it all installed a few months ago, after…" Joanna gulped convulsively and then plunged on. "After he was waiting for me in my garage that night. While I know the experience I survived biases how I view strangers, and probably will for the rest of my life, my therapist told me it was crucial I decide upon the limits his attack put on my life. I elected to take control over my safety in my own home by installing this gear." She ran her fingers along the arm of the couch. "I'd always felt safe here until that night.

"Even though some people might think I've given into fear with this system, I can choose who is allowed near me. *I* can choose," she reiterated, staring at Emily as if challenging her.

"I congratulate you on taking such positive measures, Ms. Halton. You've successfully taken back something your attacker tried to steal from you—your peace of mind. It's a sad fact of life that we all have to live in some kind of fortress these days. We have to watch where we park, who is near us and where we walk in the evening.

"And you know, you're right. It *is* up to you whom you allow into your home and under what conditions. I think it's much better to select those you allow into your life than to retreat from life altogether. Don't you agree?" Emily asked with a smile.

Obviously relieved, Joanna seemed to relax as she nodded and returned the young detective's smile. "May I offer you some coffee?" Joanna turned to a carafe on the side table.

"Please. I take mine with cream and sugar."

"A cop who doesn't take it black and strong?" Joanna was smiling openly now.

"What can I say? I don't even like donuts," Emily confessed with a chuckle. "After ten years on the force, you'd think I'd have developed a taste for them by now, wouldn't you?"

As Joanna poured generous mugs of coffee for each of them, Emily mentally reviewed the details of Joanna's case. Joanna was an attorney on the fast track to partnership in one of Yorkton's most renowned firms. She was not, however, in the dangerous world of criminal defense where a convicted client could prove deadly. Joanna assembled corporations and, by all accounts, was very good at complex international negotiations.

She dealt in stock options, not prison terms.

The young attorney had never married, but had ended a relationship with a surgeon in a neighboring community shortly before her assault. Neither had taken it hard. Both were busy, working on building careers important to them. Even so, the police had thoroughly investigated the former boyfriend. Ultimately, they'd been satisfied he had not been involved in Joanna's assault.

Joanna had arrived home at ten o'clock after taking clients to dinner that Tuesday evening. She'd pulled into her driveway, hit the button to open her garage door, driven in and hit the button to close the door behind her. When she stepped out of her car inside the secured garage, she had been assaulted and raped by an unknown man who had been waiting behind a old dresser stored in a corner.

"Your coffee, Detective Evans." Joanna held out a mug to her. "Detective Evans?"

With a jolt, Emily returned to the present. "Thank you." She accepted the cup and sipped it appreciatively. "And please, call me Emily. Detective Evans makes me feel so, I don't know, I guess 'official' would be the word I'm looking for. This is police business, but tonight's discussion is more information gathering, really. Not like the formal interview you had with Detectives Jorgensen and Scott when you first reported the attack."

"Emily, then. And I'd like you to call me Joanna."

"Before we start, Joanna, I want you to know I do have a sense of the abhorrence and outrage you must still feel. While I've never been violated in such an assault, my sister, Rowena, was a model on assignment in New Orleans when she was raped and murdered. I had to go down there and identify her body." Emily paused and swallowed. "Her attacker was never found. I can empathize with the fear and the anger you've lived with since that night."

"Oh, Emily, I'm so sorry to hear about your sister."

"Thank you. And know how much I appreciate you going over this again. Because if what I suspect is true, your help is invaluable to me."

"What do you mean by what you suspect?"

Emily looked staunchly at the young lawyer sitting across from her. "I believe there's a serial rapist in Yorkton."

Joanna gasped.

Emily continued. "And more than that, I suspect he's choosing his targets very carefully. This isn't random crime. I don't believe this guy just happened to be lurking in your garage on that Tuesday night and then decided to molest you when you arrived home."

"You mean it's somebody I know?" Joanna was obviously horrified at the thought.

"I don't mean to imply he's a co-worker or someone like that," Emily was quick to reassure her. "But I do presume you've come into contact with him in some way, somewhere before the night he raped you."

"But then wouldn't I have recognized him?"

"Well, that's what we need to go over."

Carefully, Emily led Joanna back to the night of her rape and they reconstructed the episode in detail. By the time they were done, the coffee pot had been refilled and every facet of Joanna's ordeal had been scrutinized by the two of them. At times, Joanna succumbed to tears and self-recrimination. Emily reassured the young woman she'd done nothing wrong and hadn't invited the attack in any way.

What Emily learned from Joanna assured her she was, indeed, on the right track in her burgeoning search for the gruesome trail of a serial rapist. Too many of the details were eerily similar to those Angela had recounted about her friend, Jen's, rape. And, disturbingly, each had had a lock of hair trimmed after the rape.

"I thought the scissors were to stab me," confessed Joanna, "so I closed my eyes. I didn't want to see it coming. But I heard a snipping sound beside my left ear, and then he was gone, leaving me on the concrete floor beside my car. My hands were taped together right down to the tips of my fingers."

"He's collecting his own evidence," whispered Emily in triumph. "When we find him, we'll be able to convict him based on the souvenirs he's taken from each assault. Question is, has he only committed crimes here in Yorkton, or other towns and cities as well?"

Joanna shuddered. "This guy is spooky. And you think I've met this lunatic somewhere before? I don't know anybody like that. I'm sure I'd be able to spot such weird behavior."

"Oh, don't be misled. You won't see that conduct in his everyday life, Joanna. He'll be very circumspect and low key. He'll be the guy no one would ever suspect of a crime."

"Great. I might be seeing him every day at work or at the gym."

"I really don't think so. I presume this guy chooses his marks outside his everyday realm of relationships. There's less chance of random recognition that way, you see. He can commit his invasion of your life, then just walk away without ever worrying about whether you'll point the finger at him over the coffee pot in the lunch room."

"That's a relief."

"Hey," said Emily suddenly, "you remember the surgeon you dated?"

"You mean George Edwards?"

"Yeah. Just out of curiosity, how did you meet him?"

"Strange as it may seem," Joanna said with a short chuckle, "we met through the personal ads."

"The personals?" Emily's heart rate increased.

"Yeah, you know. Single white female, mid-thirties, busy and ambitious, looking for similar, non-smoking, single man who loves long summer walks on the beach and cozy winter nights in front of the fireplace."

"I know what you mean, but isn't that an incredibly risky way to meet men? How did you know this surgeon wasn't Jack the Ripper when you first met?"

"For one thing, you don't invite the people you meet through the personals to your home. You meet them someplace public like a restaurant or a coffee bar until you get to know them. Or you double date with people you know for the first few dates. Plus I only advertised in the personals section in the *Yorkton Daily Gazette*. It's a pretty upscale paper."

"Which any person, nice or not, can buy for less than fifty cents an edition," Emily admonished.

"A few friends of mine had tried it successfully, so I gave it a go. It seemed pretty safe. I mean, your real name and address aren't in the ad. The newspaper guarantees your privacy that way. They have everything set up through mail drop boxes at the paper and, if someone sends you something really bizarre, you just report it to the editor. His name is Mac something."

"Mac Landon," supplied Emily quietly.

"I hear he's a great looking guy. He's tall with these incredible eyes and dark hair. He looks like he works out, too. He's got that, you know, strong, intelligent look like he could make love to you all night and quote Keats. I never talked to him myself, but a friend of mine had to report some weirdo who kept sending naked pictures of himself to her post office box at the paper. She told me all about Mac. She'd have gone out with him in a minute. Anyway, he took care of her problem with the weirdo right away."

"Mac's not the kind of person who'd let something like that go," agreed Emily.

"He wouldn't have to stalk someone is all I meant."

"This rapist may not have to stalk anyone either. He just may get his kicks from it." Emily looked at her watch. "Wow, it's after midnight! I really appreciate how tough it was for you to do this, Joanna. But it's by going through every case detail by detail like this that we're going to catch this guy. He may think he's left no clues behind with no fingerprints or DNA evidence, but already we've discovered he's a planner and has a memento fetish."

Joanna nodded.

"And I have every intention of bringing him to justice." Emily stood up and folded shut Joanna's file.

"Thank you," said Joanna fervently as she stood up, too. Suddenly she stepped forward and gathered Emily into a gigantic hug. "Somehow, I feel like tonight is the start of the nightmare ending. I know you'll catch this guy and when you do, I want to know."

Emily nodded, moved by the other woman's courage.

*   *   *

When Emily got home, she was too keyed up by the evening's interview to sleep. She piled all eight files on her dining room table and reviewed each one again. By the time fatigue dragged down her lids, she had noted that no one, except Jen, had been attacked in a place where women were traditionally on guard against such an assault like a parking lot or a dimly-lit area. Two had been raped in their homes, two had been molested in their garages, three in their personal offices and one in the locker room of her private club. The trail to the perpetrator was far from clear. Exhausted, Emily left her notes and the files on the table and headed to bed.

The next morning, she carried her toast and tea into the dining room, drawn to the files like a magnet pulled her. As she munched, she looked through them for what seemed like the hundredth time in the last couple of days.

That's when it leapt at her like a laser. Most of the women had reported a fairly recent break-up with a boyfriend. Each had professed there'd been no hard feelings on either side. Emily skipped to the investigating officers' notes. Each time, the officers had talked to the ex-boyfriend on the phone because he either lived in a neighboring town or traveled on business. Always, the investigators had concluded that the ex-boyfriend was neither angry nor vengeful, but rather, seemed upset and horrified over what had happened to a woman he knew.

Emily sensed that if she let her subconscious work, she might identify the direction to take. She put the files into her briefcase and headed to the police station.

After touching base with Ryan and Angela, she started compiling a list of the women's former boyfriends.

Suddenly, an idea struck her.

She called Joanna at work. "Joanna, I know you told me your ex-boyfriend's name was George Edwards and that he was a surgeon from a nearby city. What city was that?"

"Smistown. Why?"

"Did he ever say which hospital he worked at or give you his work number?"

"As a matter of fact, no, he didn't. He told me his chief of staff, a Dr. Singh, was insane about employees, even surgeons, taking personal calls so he always called me if we wanted to talk during the day. I gave his home number to the detectives who investigated."

"Yep, I've got it here." Emily flipped through the file to the report.

"Smistown only has a couple of hospitals, so you could probably track him down. I never thought too much about it because he would call me a couple of times a week. I'm usually pretty busy here, so I don't have much time for talking to boyfriends on the phone. Besides we'd see each other in the evenings whenever our schedules allowed."

"Thanks, Joanna. Now, I only have one more question."

"Shoot."

"What does Dr. Edwards look like?"

"Well, he's pretty tall. I guess around six feet or thereabouts. He's in good shape. He plays squash three times a week and weight trains in between." She laughed. "He always said it makes surgery easier when he's in condition."

"So, you'd describe him as around six feet tall with a slim but muscular build?"

"Sounds right." Joanna paused. "Emily, there's just no way he's your rapist. George was a great guy. And, besides, our relationship was already intimate."

"With your consent at those times, I presume? He never forced you to have sex with him, did he? Suggested you play sex games you weren't comfortable with?"

"Never. Our relationship was quite physical as a matter of fact. Besides, he was playing squash with a colleague at the racquet club at the time I was raped. Your detectives verified that with the club."

"I think I'm going to do more digging. Talk to you later."

When Emily got off the phone, Ryan and Angela were still hard at work contacting the rest of the women. She decided to check out George Edwards of Smistown. She called the number listed as Edwards' home phone. She wasn't surprised when a recording notified her the number was no longer in service.

When the other two officers had finished talking to the rest of the women, they congregated at Emily's desk to compare notes. Every one of the victims' former boyfriends had held excellent jobs, but were difficult to reach at work, either because of a demanding boss or schedule. Each was described as being about six feet tall with a slim, muscular physique. They had all met through the personal ads.

Emily's adrenaline surged as she ordered her task force to dig deeper into each ex-boyfriend's background and alibi for the times of the attacks. By the end of the day, it was discovered that the phone numbers given for every ex-boyfriend had been disconnected. There were other inconsistencies, too. In Joanna's case, Smistown General Hospital had indeed employed a Dr. George Edwards, but he had retired several years ago and now spent much of his time at the racquet club and the country club. Also the real Dr. Edwards was five foot eight.

The identities for the rest of the ex-boyfriends were equally mysterious. The names were real and each still were or had been employed where each ex had claimed to have worked. But when they were contacted at work, a place the previous investigators had never called, they all said the same thing—not one of them had dated any of the women who claimed to know them.

Emily sensed she was on the right path. The warped miscreant had laid careful cover, but he'd made mistakes. She would use them to track him down and end his reign of cruelty.

This is one rapist who will not walk away from the charges for lack of meticulous police work. No defense attorney will find any reason to throw out even the tiniest scrap of our work.

She carefully documented their research.

* * *

Carelessly, he brushed aside the replies that had once been so intriguing. They flew off the desk and scattered on the floor. He hadn't a second thought for them. While he heard their silent pleas for his notice, he ignored them. He'd found his next consort on that elevator. She would be, he believed, his most tempting prey yet.

She had come to him. She was meant for him.

This one he would date just long enough to get her to trust him. This time, he would not enjoy her body until after he had ended the relationship, he decided.

He felt himself swell when he thought about their time together after their break-up. Those big green eyes would widen in fear at what she anticipated him doing to her against her will. But, in order to save her life, she would fulfill his every desire just as the others had. And when he demanded she beg him to perform the perverse acts he'd chosen, her enticing mouth would comply. He could almost hear her distinctive voice imploring him to violate her.

He could hardly wait.

CHAPTER 5

Emily slapped at the clock radio, but the resounding noise didn't stop. She forced one eye open. It was fifteen minutes before her alarm was even due to go off. For the past two nights, she'd worked late on the rape case. Now, she intended to sleep as long as possible. The electronic ring jabbed her ears once more before she realized it was her phone. She stretched out her hand and snagged the receiver.

"What do you want?" Emily didn't even pretend to be friendly. The department knew better than to call her early in the morning unless it was an emergency. Family wouldn't awaken her unless someone was hospitalized.

"Just to say good morning." Mac's voice was cheerful and too wide awake to be real at this hour.

"Good morning," she growled and dropped the receiver into the cradle.

She'd scarcely had time to roll back onto her tummy before the ringing started again. She snatched up the receiver, but before she had time to utter a word, he spoke.

"If I come bearing croissants and English breakfast tea in about half an hour, would you be conscious?" He'd toned down his early morning energy.

"Make it forty-five minutes and I'll even have my hair combed." A smile crossed her face before she could stop it. "But I can't promise I'll be as wide awake as you seem to be in the middle of the night." With a chuckle, she hung up. She was beaming as she headed for the shower.

*   *   *

Her laughter undid him. Mac set down the phone and dropped into a chair. He couldn't believe his reaction to her sleep-flooded words. If he'd thought her voice was sexy during a business meeting, it was absolutely beguiling when she was still drowsy.

His heart pounded heavily in his chest. He could fight toe to toe in budget battles with hardened publishers with nary a ripple of emotion. Yet now, a crowd of butterflies had invaded his stomach. This woman had entered his life less than three days ago, and he found himself overwhelmed by emotions he'd carefully built barriers against throughout the years After only one meeting with Emily, those barricades had crashed to the ground in a heap of useless rubble. She had touched his core without even trying to. Through her, he'd discovered the other half of himself. It was a portion he'd not even known was missing until she'd walked calmly into his office, undismayed by his façade of cold anger.

She fascinated him.

He pictured Emily groping for her bedside phone, dazed with sleep. Mac longed to run his fingers through that soft tangle of wild, auburn hair. He imagined its silky passage across the naked skin of his chest as she leaned down to kiss his mouth good morning.

Mac fantasized about trailing tiny kisses across the lids of those huge emerald eyes to awaken her gently. He wanted Emily's eyes to widen in joy as he adored her with his mouth, his hands and his maleness. He craved the sight of her strong, lithe body responding to him. He yearned to hear that low-timbered voice breathe his name as he followed her over the edge of passion.

For a few more minutes, Mac indulged in the mental imagery of making love to this intriguing woman who was braver than anyone he'd ever met. But fantasies were not enough. He intended to make her his. Yet, he realized winning her over was not like the other conquests he'd experienced.

And now, even before he'd completely won her over, Mac risked losing her. His soul staggered at the fear he felt for her safety. He had to dissuade her from taking the course of action she was contemplating; action that exposed her to mortal danger. Because he realized that if she set herself up as bait, this particular hunter would find the trail she laid down for him. Emily would prove irresistible to him and he'd pursue her without exhausting of the chase in order to drag her into his world of abasement. Mac knew this as clearly as if the man had spoken to him.

He also understood that no matter what happened, Emily would never submit to the rapist's diseased nightmare of control and submission. And that could cost Emily her life.

There had to be another way to stop this rapist. Not that Mac believed Emily would abandon her pursuit of the stalker, altogether. Her nucleus of courage, earned at unbelievable expense, wouldn't permit her to back off from the crusade. Still, there were ways to reduce the risks for her.

Mac hoped to convince Emily to let him participate in the hunt. But his manner of offering this suggestion had to be just right. He certainly couldn't take a macho approach with her. She might receive the mistaken impression he thought her less than capable. Above all, he'd have to rein in his deep feelings for Emily so they couldn't prejudice his normally rational ability to strategize while negotiating.

Mac was still considering the best way of working out the situation with Emily when he pulled into her driveway. He glanced down at his watch. It was exactly forty-five minutes since he'd talked to her on the phone. He couldn't contain his grin as he anticipated his welcome. Would she be up yet, or had she rolled over and fallen back to sleep? He really didn't care. If he had to, he'd find a way to gently rouse her. He leaned over and scooped up the newspaper from the front step. His newspaper.

He had to ring the bell twice before the door opened.

"Talk about delivery service." She smiled, taking the paper from him. "What day do you come around to collect?"

Emily overwhelmed him.

"I plan to collect right now." Without having planned it, Mac leaned forward and kissed her warm lips, still slightly parted from her smile. He tasted her response as she leaned against him and tentatively touched his inner lower lip with her tongue. He reacted instantly and his hardness pressed intimately against her belly below the satin robe she had belted around her.

Afraid of moving too fast and frightening her off, Mac reluctantly broke the embrace. It was one of the most difficult things he'd ever done.

She stepped back and he followed her inside the house. He held the large paper bag with their tea and croissants discreetly in front of himself as he trailed her to the kitchen.

Bright morning sunshine drenched the room with light and touched the slight color in her cheeks—the result of their encounter at the front door. Emily busied herself with cups, saucers and plates for their impromptu breakfast. Mac sat back and enjoyed the view.

I'd love to watch this woman every morning.

The thought surprised him as he watched her setting out the dishes, enchanting him with the everyday routine of the task. Her bright hair was pulled up in a large hair clip allowing a few tendrils to curl about her face. Her satin robe swayed and slid against her long legs, silhouetting them. He caught a glimpse of lace where the robe opened and felt heat rise in him again. Mac shifted his focus, studying her hands as she worked. The long, slim fingers were magic to behold and his thoughts were no more chaste than they had been a few moments earlier.

"Do you take cream or lemon with your tea, Mac?" Even nearly an hour later her voice was still reminiscent of time spent in bed.

"Cream," he managed. "Can I do anything to help?"

"No. I think bringing breakfast is enough. The least I can do is get out the dishes."

* * *

She had to keep busy or else she'd push the cutlery and dishes to the floor and throw herself on the table, hoping he'd ravish her right there. Emily couldn't stop the blush staining her cheeks. If he only knew how much time she'd spent dabbing on perfume, fussing with her hair until the tendrils drifted by her face perfectly and tossing everything out of her lingerie drawer until she found the one silk chemise she owned. Somehow, she would manage to "let" him notice the way the silk clung to her body.

She looked up to see Mac staring at her. Suddenly, she felt she could read his thoughts. He was experiencing the same sensation she was. Her face grew warmer. Never before had she been so attracted to a man.

In fact, over the past few years, she'd rarely dated, let alone considered intimacy with someone. Especially with someone she'd met only a few days before. This was the new millennium and Emily was neither stupid nor naive. She didn't know a thing about Mac's sexual history and didn't plan to take a risk.

He was speaking in a hoarse voice. "I can't believe what you do to me, Emily. Just watching you set the table takes my breath away. I haven't been with anyone for a long time. Yet now, all I can think about is clearing the table and making love to you right here."

"Well, Mac"—she looked up from under lowered lashes—"I was considering getting rid of the dishes, myself. But I need to know you better. I hope you understand."

"Of course."

"Good. But if I'm as honest with you as you were with me, I'm going to admit that I was having—shall we call them lascivious—thoughts about you the other morning in your office. And again this morning." Emily took a deep breath. "This isn't my usual style, Mac. It really isn't. There's just something about you and my reaction to you."

"Like you've known me all your life and have been waiting for me to show up?"

"Yeah, that's it exactly. It's as if I know how you think."

"Really?" He grinned lewdly at her.

"Yes." She wiggled her eyebrows at him. But when she spoke, her tone was serious. "Which is why I understand this morning's breakfast is your way of trying to deter me from answering replies to my ad."

"I wouldn't be truthful if I said you were wrong, but"—he paused, holding up his hand palm outward—"what I'm really here to do is offer my help."

"Your help?"

"I'm not a police officer, but I've dealt with a few screwballs over the years, and before I became managing editor here, I covered the city beat in Detroit. I know how to talk to people, and how to intimidate them when necessary."

"I think I was given a dose of Mac Landon coercion the first day we met, wasn't I?" Emily asked with a grin.

"Well, it's worked on lots of other people over the years."

"Really, Mac, I'd love to involve you, but this is a police operation, and we plan to land on this guy hard."

"I don't plan to interfere in what you're doing. But I could monitor your mailbox at the paper to watch for anything unusual in the replies you get. Don't forget, I'm an expert in the personals and may have a different view than even your police psychologist."

"Okay." She capitulated with a smile. "It'd be great to have you on my team. But don't think you can distract me," she warned with a wave of her forefinger.

* * *

He nodded in relief. And least he could be close to her, and might even have a chance to protect her from the ravenous monster who would soon pursue her. It was all he could do for the moment.

Mac smiled gently at Emily as he passed her the strawberry jam. He just prayed she would be as careful as she promised.

A sudden thought occurred to him. “You said you’re working with a task force, right?”

“Yep, besides me, Angela O’Connell and Ryan James are working this detail with me. Oh, and the police psychologist, Barbara Totten.”

“Is there a reason why, when you go out with the men you pick out as potential rapists, we can’t divide up into two other couples and be at whatever coffee shop or restaurant you plan to meet him?”

Emily smiled and the kitchen glimmered more brightly. “Now you’re even starting to sound like a cop. We’ve already worked out a backup scheme so I’ll never be alone with any of these guys. And it’s going to be good duty for those who participate.”

“Why?”

“Our victims have been upscale professionals. They don’t go to McDonald’s or Burger King on their dates. No, sir, Mr. Fancy Managing Editor.” Another grin delighted him. “I’ll be dining at Dante’s or going to the theater followed by dessert and coffee at Cappuccino Cream. No budget dates for this little undercover cop. In fact, Angela says that if the operation goes on longer than a week, her husband is going to want on the team.” She looked at him mischievously. “For my part, I kinda think it’ll make up for the times I’ve had to pose as a hooker down by the docks.”

He suddenly realized what she’d said. “Hey, there are no docks in Yorkton. We’re landlocked.”

“Gotcha.”

“Gotcha back,” he murmured as he reached across the table and stroked his finger softly across her cheek. “Just be careful and I mean it. I’ve been looking for you my whole life. Now that I’ve found you, I want to get to know you a whole lot better.”

Emily smiled as she captured his hand and tenderly kissed his palm. “Come on, Mac, I’ve got a long day ahead of me and so do you.”

“Yeah,” he said as he leaned across the table. “But I need something to sustain me through that day,” he murmured before he captured her mouth.

* * *

His frustration had finally abated. Yesterday, he’d been unable to get the information he wanted. That damned Amanda had worked at her desk all day, even through lunch. He could have wrung her neck when she’d asked him to get her a sandwich at noon. The woman hadn't even taken a coffee break. Then, when he'd returned after dark, all the day's copy was already gone from her work basket and he couldn't access her computer. What *was* her new password, anyway?

A white hot torrent of anger had almost flared out of control as Amanda chirped a bright "hello" when she arrived this morning. What he'd like to do to her for standing in his way yesterday! He'd clasped his hands together under his desk to keep from reaching for her throat.

But Amanda inadvertently saved herself from his rage. She signed onto her computer immediately, and then offered to get him a cup of coffee when she got her own.

"You were so nice to me yesterday when I was so far behind." She smiled at him, unable to see his hidden fury. "The least I can do is get you coffee this morning."

Rage evaporated as he agreed, knowing she'd be gone for a few minutes. He would arouse no suspicions if he worked at her terminal pretending to be taking an ad over the phone. Delighted at the opportunity, he quickly copied the files of all the personals Amanda had worked on yesterday afternoon. He pocketed the diskette, so pleased with his feat that when Amanda returned, he offered to take her to lunch at her favorite deli.

Now, he was finally alone at his desk and could slip the diskette into his briefcase. He'd had to copy more files of stolen information than he needed and it would take time to sort through it tonight, but that didn't matter.

He would find her.

She was so close, the scent of her trail engulfed him. He sniffed the air greedily. He would have her real name and address within minutes of loading the diskette into his home computer. Later this evening he would compose his reply to her ad. Then he would gain physical access to her, and it would be through an avenue she expected.

He knew exactly what she needed to hear. She'd want him to be sensitive, caring and compassionate. He could be all of those things for as long as it took to lull her into a sense of safety.

Maybe she was the one he'd been thinking about for some time, the one he'd been searching for. She was the embodiment of all that would challenge his abilities. Exceptionally attractive…fit…his mastery of her would be his ultimate triumph.

Maybe he would cage her, keep her for a while, sampling her several times. It would mean changing his tactic of striking once and leaving no clues behind.

He bared his teeth. Finding prey had become too easy over the years. He felt the need to challenge himself ripple through his psyche. Now was the time to prove himself again.

She would be worth the risk.

CHAPTER 6

Emily and Dr. Barbara Totten sat in the conference room staring at the towering pile of mail on the table before them. In just the few days since Emily's ad had run in *The Daily Gazette,* dozens of replies had poured in. Most came in regular, white business size, but a number of large manila envelopes with "Photos—Do Not Bend" penned across them had also arrived. It was time to start analyzing them.

"Wow." Emily looked in dismay at the letters. "This is going to take some time. I thought I'd just get one or two a day. I figured Angela and I would start dating these people right away."

"Your ad was designed to attract attention, Emily, so don't be surprised by a large volume of mail. Your target will be somewhere in these piles, you can count on it. If not today, then soon. Remember how we chose key words calculated to appeal to the profile we've worked up on this guy."

Their profile consisted of several key characteristics. The suspect thought himself smarter than others. He had little or no respect for women, but liked tricking them into trusting him by the use of romance and pretending to hold an upscale job. He pretended to care about the bright, successful woman upon whom he preyed.

The advertisement composed by the task force appealed to these traits: "Searching for a kindred soul to share relaxing moments in the sun and quiet romantic evenings together. Single white female, non-smoker, on a quest for the perfect gentleman to complete her already abundant life."

Barbara had explained to Emily that through this personal ad, their suspect would see her as a romantic, hoping to find a man to court and woo her gently. She should expect candlelight dinners, an evening at the ballet, theater or opera. He'll take her on a dawn or sunset walk during which he'll describe his perfect childhood growing up on Cape Cod or the beaches of California with his Golden Retriever ever by his side.

The psychologist warned Emily not to fall for the rapist's manipulation. "He needs and wants you to buy into his fantasy. It's what gives him the control he craves. Remember, his fantasy is the gentle woman who is at his beck and call, to abuse as he sees fit."

Emily sighed, as she thought of the challenge before her, then glanced up to see Barbara watching her. A worried expression stretched across the psychologist's face. Barbara was a woman who knew her inside and out, the one who'd helped her through the nightmares following Rowena's death. Emily reached out and covered the woman's hand with her own. "Don't think I'll forget for even one second why I'm doing this—or who I'm searching for, Barbara."

"Good, because if you forget while you're with this guy, I mean even for a moment, he'll be taking a lock of your hair to add to his collection before you know what hit you. I don't want you or Angela to become the next victim of this sick bastard."

"Neither do I," agreed Emily, her voice grim.

Angela and Ryan arrived at that moment and stared at the mountain of mail waiting for them to dissect.

"Got time to grab some coffee while we work on this?" Ryan's voice was as hopeful as his expression. His tall, rangy frame made him look younger than he was.

"Sure," replied Emily.

"Hey, Detective James, make mine double sugar and cream," piped up the super-slender Angela, "and grab me a donut or muffin if there're any left."

"Anybody else?" asked Ryan with a grin, looking around the room.

"I'll take mine with cream and sugar," answered Emily.

"And just a bit of sweetener in mine," chimed in the psychologist.

While their colleague gathered coffee and snacks, the women divided the mail into two piles. One stack consisted of envelopes obviously containing photos, the other correspondence only. Emily eyed the larger envelopes with curiosity. It took a certain boldness to send an unsolicited photo of one's self to a stranger. Then again, she wasn't searching for a shrinking violet, but a man who terrorized women with whom he'd already formed a relationship.

When Ryan returned and the coffee was distributed, they got down to the business of finding their hunter.

They knew immediately the first letter was not sent by the man for whom they searched. Lester described himself as an excellent cook who had won prizes for his azaleas at the local fair and had a small menagerie of cats and birds.

"This actually sounds like a form letter," murmured Angela. "He didn't even bother to address it to your assigned personals code number, just 'Dear Lady Love.' Wonder how many dates he's gotten over the years with this?"

"Well, it must be reasonably successful or surely Lester would've tried another strategy," retorted Emily. "I'm sure he's not our target. This guy seems to be looking for a date, not a victim. There's nothing of a romantic fantasy in any of this. It's sweet and down home but definitely not calculated to have someone swooning."

"I don't think dinner and a movie with Emily are going to be in his plans," said Angela glancing around the table. Emily and Barbara nodded their agreement. Lester's letter was laid on a side table.

Emily picked up another envelope and slit it open. A hand-printed note tumbled onto the conference table's scarred wooden surface. "Here's an unusual choice," said Emily. "Hand printed. Not writing, but not childish either."

"Could be a very creative type—perhaps in advertising or media," counseled Barbara. "You know, someone accustomed to having his ideas stand out in a crowd. He'd want you to notice his letter immediately."

"I think he might be worth considering," said Angela thoughtfully. "What does his note say, Emily?"

"'Love quiet times and gourmet food. Not looking to settle down to suburban lifestyle, but interested in a long term relationship with the right woman. If you're independent and original, I'd love to get together for an evening of exploring whether we might be right for one another.' And then he leaves his phone number. It's local." She looked around the table. "It's printed, but with a fountain pen. I agree with Angela, this one's definitely worth tracking."

Emily tossed the note into the center of the conference table. The room was silent for a few moments as everyone sorted through the remaining letters.

"Here's another one that might fit our profile." Ryan read from a sheet of heavy, cream-colored bond paper. "'I've been waiting for you. And finally I found your message. You sound like my soul mate. I must meet you and you must meet me. Please contact me and let's join our lives.' It's signed 'Jonas' with no last name. He gives an e-mail address."

"Let's add him to the list of possible candidates," said Barbara emphatically. "There's a need for control in his letter, and an archaic style in the way he refers to joining your lives. I'd say Jonas is worth a second look."

* * *

Slowly they worked through the remainder of the letters. After a few hours, they had four possible candidates including one who'd sent a photo. Each of the men had included a contact phone number, except Jonas and his e-mail address.

"Well, I guess we'd better start making calls," Emily said. "You got all the recording equipment set up, Ryan?"

"Sure do. The doc here will be able to analyze everything each one says to you. We'll nail this guy no matter what."

"Okay, let's get to it." Emily nodded to Angela. "Take your pick and you can make the first call if you want."

Angela beamed. "Thanks, Emily, I'd love to." She shuffled through the letters and pulled out the one with the photo. "This guy, Brent, intrigues me. Shall I set up dinner?"

"Remember, don't be too anxious to go out right away," advised Dr. Totten. "We want him to pursue you a bit and see how he handles the stalking part of this game. Our rapist will enjoy the hunt almost as much as the capture, I believe. He may even want to enhance his anticipation by delaying a date."

Angela nodded. "I'll play along with what he says. Maybe even suggest we take it slow, and see what he does with that."

"Good idea. Just be careful not to betray any details about your real life," coached Emily.

The other three listened carefully as Angela threaded her way through the conversation with Brent, finally agreeing to meet him for dinner at Breadstix. The task force had decided every date would take place at the trendy restaurant because it provided an environment in which the police could provide back-up that would go unnoticed by the target.

"Only problem is," grumbled Angela as she hung up, "we're not going out 'til next Saturday night."

"But you played it perfectly," said Emily. "You came across as reluctant, but interested. And most of all, you didn't sound desperate. If this is our guy, he's not interested in easy. He wants his conquest to be challenging."

"True enough."

"And remember, this gives him nearly a week to prepare and plan his tactics. You'll have to be very careful with him, Angela," warned the psychologist.

Ryan set down his cup and looked around the room. "I don't think this is our guy. I really don't."

"Reason?" asked Emily.

"I didn't hear an undertone. I think he's conceited, and his ego isn't the least of his problems, but I can't hear any hunter quality to his speech patterns or his attitude. He obviously isn't being open, but then again he may be married or involved." He picked up his cup and swirled the remnants of coffee slowly. "I can't find anything in his approach to Angela that tells me he's a serial rapist stalking a victim. And I really don't think our guy is going to wait nearly a week to begin his game of cat and mouse."

"I'd agree with you from this first conversation with him," said Dr. Totten easily. "But we've got to treat each date as if he is the one we're looking for. He will be very careful even though he considers himself superior. Let's keep going. We still have a few more to try."

The afternoon drifted by as they pursued their options. The four carefully composed a reply e-mail with a dummy return address to Jonas, setting up a dinner meeting at Breadstix with Emily. It was only a few minutes before his message flashed back agreeing to meet the following Tuesday at seven-thirty. He'd wear a navy suit and meet her by the indoor fountain.

Emily was also booked for an evening out with Chris. He'd identified himself as a poet who supported himself as a computer programmer with a major player in the industry. They'd also be meeting at Breadstix, but it would be for lunch on Monday. Emily agreed to meet him at a table overlooking the pond behind the restaurant. She was to check in with the maitre d' by twelve-fifteen and let him seat her. Chris would meet her there by twelve-thirty.

"Doesn't sound much like a control freak, does he?" said Emily and laughed. "This guy sure likes to set the rules."

"Yes, he does," agreed Barbara. "Why don't we give him a bit of rope at lunch and see how controlling he wants to be?"

"I get the feeling Chris would like total control," Emily replied, looking around the table. "Anyone disagree?"

"No way," retorted Angela. "He told you when and where. I'm surprised he didn't tell you to wear a red rose in your hair. I'll bet he even orders for you. Hope he's not dumb enough to pick veal." She laughed. "He won't stand a chance in hell then."

"Well," Ryan said before he sipped the last of his cold coffee. "At least he didn't object when Emily suggested Breadstix. I was kind of worried he would, just on principle."

"I could feel him getting ready to object," Emily said. "That's why I really deferred to him. If *he* wanted to go to Breadstix, I'd love to go since I'd never been there even though some of my girlfriends have talked about how great it is."

"Just don't underestimate that kind of person's need to maintain control," counseled Barbara. "It's very important to them."

"Hey, how about my date tonight with Gord?" asked Angela. "Anybody get any funny feelings about him?"

"I thought he made a couple of references that seemed a bit off." Ryan forwarded the tape he'd made of the conversation, then slipped on the headphones and made another adjustment. "Here it is. I knew I'd marked the tape right." He took off the earphones and raised the volume on speakers of such high quality, even background noise was audible.

A slightly nasal voice filled the room. "Well, things can get pretty cut-throat in the numbers game, but I don't miss too many signs when I'm on the trail of a new stock."

"He was talking about the financial markets, though," Emily remarked. "Those guys tend to think of themselves in pretty wolfish terms. It keeps them bouyed up."

"True," said Barbara, "but speech patterns can betray a person's real personality. Let's just take it really careful tonight with Gord. Okay, Angela?" She looked at the young detective. "I don't want your first stake out to be your last." The psychologist's remarks dampened the mood in the room. "I'm sure you realize the guy we're after is deadly serious about this. It's not a game to him. It's how he views his relationship with women. It's how he views himself in life—as the victor physically and psychologically. He must maintain that image of himself at any cost. He's gotten used to doing just that. And you two," she gazed at Emily and Angela, "have deliberately put yourselves in harm's way."

"Barbara," Emily touched the other woman's arm gently, "we're also police officers, well-trained in both self-defense and how to bring down a violent perpetrator. We've spent time on the street and cleared out our share of drunk and disorderly patrons from downtown bars."

She looked around at the others. "I, for one, am smarter and better prepared than this guy ever expects. And there's not going to be one moment I'm not acutely aware of what he plans to do to me if he gets control of me. I believe Angela is similarly prepared." She looked at her colleague who nodded solemnly. "Good, because we've got a job to do. And with Angela's date, it starts to roll tonight."

"We're set to meet at Breadstix at seven-thirty."

Emily glanced down at her watch. "It's nearly four o'clock now. Why don't you head over to the motor pool and check out a car, Angela. I don't want anyone getting a license number from your own vehicle. Then you might as well go home and get ready. When you see Ryan and me at the restaurant, don't even give a hint you know us. Pretend you've never been there before. We want Gord to think he has you on unfamiliar turf."

Angela nodded and headed out of the room. Ryan gathered his tapes and meticulously logged them for evidence should they be needed during a trial.

Barbara smiled at Emily as she closed her file folders and tucked them into her briefcase. "Emily, I don't think I've ever seen you stronger."

"I appreciate that, but I won't feel I've done my job 'til this lowlife is behind bars." Her voice was steel and her eyes met her friend's with resolve. "Without your help Barbara, I wouldn't be here to do this job."

"I'm pretty sure you would be, Emily. You just needed my help to see your grief wasn't anger and it didn't need to be self-directed. You're the only person who could handle this assignment the way it needs to be handled—with empathy and detachment coupled with a complete understanding of what this crime does to a victim."

"Thanks." Emily reached for her ringing phone. "Evans here." She tucked the phone between her shoulder and ear and waved to the departing Dr. Totten.

"Hi there, morning girl."

Emily couldn't have stopped the smile that broke across face if she'd wanted to. "Mac, how's it going?"

"Good. Just wondered if you wanted to have dinner together. I sure enjoyed starting the day with breakfast with you. Thought it might be a nice way to end the day—together, that is. Not with breakfast."

Her smile bubbled into laughter. This man had a way of charming her she'd thought herself beyond. "Well, I'd love to, but I've got to work."

"First date?" She could hear the concern in his voice even as he attempted to keep the question casual.

"No, more babysitting detail really. Angela is taking the first date tonight with a guy named Gord. Ryan and I are riding shotgun."

"Room for a newspaper editor at your table?"

"Mac, sure you're a great newspaper editor. And I know you spent your share of time as a reporter covering the police beat. But the bottom line is, you're a civilian. I thought we'd been through all this." Her tone was gentle.

"We did go through this, and as I recall, you agreed to let me help."

"Help, yes. Be part of the task force, no."

"You did say I could go to the restaurant."

"Yes, I guess I did." Emily glanced up at Ryan signaling to her. "Mac, can you hold on a moment, please." She covered the mouthpiece of the phone and looked at Ryan.

"Is that Mac Landon, the managing editor over at the *Daily Gazette*?"

"Yeah, why?"

"Well, I was just thinking. Mac was the best crime reporter they ever had at that rag. There're plenty of times he protected a source and he did very pretty professional investigative reporting over the years. He helped break the crack smuggling case I worked on about five years ago. Dug up leads we never would have gotten ourselves just 'cause we're cops," Ryan said. "I trust the man. If I team up with Officer Olson and you go to Breadstix with Landon, we've got Angela covered from two angles."

"Would you be talking about Officer Megan Olson?"

"Sure." The blush rushed across his face against his will. "She's a great officer and has plenty of street experience."

"And you were planning to see her tonight, weren't you?"

"Yeah, but hey, there's no way I'd jeopardize Angela's safety. Still, wouldn't four pair of eyes watching her be better than two?" He looked at her expectantly.

"Can you keep your mind on the assignment?" Her tone was cool and professional. "This isn't a date."

"You better believe it." Ryan looked her straight in the eyes. "Megan actually has been assisting me with this when we're off duty. She's helped me see how such attacks affect women in very personal ways. Her college room mate was raped and beaten, almost to death, a few years ago."

"Okay, she's part of the team for tonight," Emily agreed. "And if Megan can give you any help, strictly off-duty and on personal time, take it. We want this sicko caught and caught soon." She took her hand off the mouthpiece. "Mac, you're part of tonight's party. Pick me up at six-thirty. We want to be there in plenty of time."

"We'll be part of the scenery by the time Angela and Gord arrive. See you at six- thirty." He hung up.

* * *

Excitement throbbed as he closed and locked the door to his apartment and jabbed in the security code. He heightened his anticipation by making himself a meal and eating it before he allowed himself the joy of finding out her name and her need. All the while, the diskette holding the key to his next victim sat on the table beside him. He could hear it whispering its secrets in a language he could decipher only at his computer.

As the sun set and shadows lengthened, he carried his prize into the dark of his den. The computer screen cast its light over his features as he began to type his letter that would lure her to him. He didn't yet know her name, but he had seen her face and her body. He bared his teeth as his fingers flew across the keyboard.

Soon he would know her. Soon he would own her.

CHAPTER 7

Emily headed for home after the task force had finalized the evening's arrangements. Emily and Mac would be at the restaurant, along with Ryan and Megan, about an hour before Angela and Gord were due to arrive. That would give them time to select strategic tables for their stake out, and to position themselves accordingly.

She smiled, admitting to herself that having four observers posted at two tables watching over Angela, and if necessary, blocking the exits, worked out even better than their previous plan. If Gord even blinked crooked, they'd take him down between the hors d'oeuvres and the salad.

Shrugging out of her work clothes, Emily padded into her custom designed bathroom. It was the one extravagance she allowed herself. She had spent considerable money creating it. She'd had the wall between her once-tiny en suite bathroom and the small fourth bedroom knocked out. And she'd had a dream bathroom installed, filled with marble and skylights and plants. The elevated bathtub, complete with whirlpool jets, took up one corner of the room. In another corner, the shower's multiple shower heads offered the ultimate in luxury. A vanity had been custom-designed. Overhead, perfect lighting glowed.

This was Emily's sanctuary and she shared it with no one.

Emily smiled as she turned the faucets to start water running into the tub. She had enough time for a twenty minute soak before she had to get ready for her evening. Her smile deepened as she opened the bottle of sunflower bath oil and drizzled it into the water. Soon, her favorite scent wafted through the room.

She slipped out of her underwear and stepped over to the vanity where she grabbed a scrunchie and pulled her hair on top of her head. Then she sank gratefully into the tub of bubbling, scented water, allowing its caressing currents to soothe her.

Emily let her mind wander away from the horror she would soon encounter, if all went according to plan. It was hard to avoid feeling the terror and pain of the women who'd been raped by the man she was hoping to attract to herself. It was harder still to avoid thoughts of her sister's pain and terror at the hands of an unknown rapist and murderer.

Emily closed her eyes with a sad sigh. "We'll stop this guy, I promise you, Rowena. He won't hurt anyone else." Tension swept over her. Then, it seemed as if an invisible hand gently stroked her hair. Her stress dissolved.

Emily lay in the water for a few more minutes as the bubbles worked their magic. When she climbed out of the tub, Emily felt rejuvenated and could hardly wait for the evening to begin. Cuddling into a full-length terry robe, she headed to her closet.

While she didn't have a lot of evening wear, she did have a knock-his-eyes-out cinnamon-colored silk sheath she loved. It just brushed her knees, skimmed over her body and was sleeveless with a modest neckline, but its daring vee-back plunged to her waist and the slit up the back of the skirt was longer than it needed to be. She always felt incredibly exotic wearing it.

She chose her only silk lingerie to wear under the dress. Pearls glowed around her neck and at her ears. Emily never knew what to do with her hair, so she brushed its wavy length until it gleamed and then twisted it up and captured in with a pearl barrette. Tendrils curled around her face accenting her eyes and softening her face's sharp planes. She coated her long lashes with mascara, dusted powder over her face and slicked on her favorite coppery lipstick. She looked in the mirror.

"There's just something about this dress." Smiling at the romantic stranger in the mirror, she slid her feet into shoes carefully chosen for their sensible flared heels. She'd need to move quickly if Gord suspected he was surrounded by police and tried to make a run for it.

The doorbell sounded and Emily took one last look in the mirror, convincing herself she'd blend in with the up and coming career women and men who frequented Breadstix. With just a hint of nervous anticipation, she opened her front door. And caught her breath.

Mac looked incredibly handsome. His dark grey suit was obviously a designer's creation, and he wore it with detached panache. His silk tie was the same thundercloud grey as his suit, with just a touch of blue running through it. The white shirt was so crisp and bright, it almost hurt the eyes. And his black leather tasseled moccasins were perfect. This was definitely a man accustomed to dressing well.

Emily smiled in pure enjoyment as she looked him over.

"Do I pass muster?" Mac grinned and executed a perfect runway turn on her front step.

"Oh, most definitely, you do indeed." Emily tilted her head and smiled teasingly. "You clean up very nicely, Mac."

"And you, my beauty, have outdone yourself," he breathed as his eyes stroked over her. "I love that dress on you. It's perfect."

"Well, come in for a few minutes," Emily invited, turning away to lead him into the living room. She heard his groan and spun.

He stared at her, passion etched clearly on his face.

"Are you all right?" she asked.

"I…I, just, ah, didn't. That is…I…I…" he stammered, stepping towards her.

"What is it?" Alarm began to build.

"The back of that dress," he swallowed, and seemed to regain control. "It's like you're naked under it."

"Well, not completely." Emily smiled.

"You might as well be. The back is unbelievable, and I can see almost the entire length of those fabulous legs when you walk away from me." He looked down at the bulge in his perfectly-fit trousers. "And what I can't see, I definitely want to see." He paused and looked at her. "And touch."

Emily might have been years beyond thinking herself capable of it, but she found herself blushing. "I'm glad you like how I look tonight."

"Hhhmmm, I wouldn't necessarily say I like it that we're going out with you wearing such a dress. I don't think I'll be the only man who notices you."

"But you're the only one I care about noticing me." The words were out before Emily could stop them. They hung in the air, as obvious as Mac's interest in her.

"Really?"

"Really." She might as well admit her growing interest. "Let's go into the living room. We don't have to leave just yet." She turned and walked away. Not hearing his footsteps behind her, she looked back from the door to the living room. “Problem?” Emily teased.

“Nope, just enjoying the view.”

In a few strides he crossed the foyer to stop in front of her, and slid his hands up the length of her sleeveless arms. Emily felt her nipples tighten and peak at his touch. She saw him look down and register her reaction, which was impossible to hide under the traitorous silk. His hands trailed back down her arms and he took her hands.

The silk was molten on her body.

Mac stepped back and dropped one of her hands, holding the other loosely as he spun her away from him until she was facing away from him. He groaned softly again and let go of her hand.

Emily stood quietly, waiting for his touch, aching to feel his hands on her. In a moment, she was rewarded.

He gently traced the edges of the vee from her shoulders to her lower back. When his fingers met at the bottom, he paused for only an instant before he splayed his hands under the silk, caressing her back.

Emily sighed in satisfaction. She’d never thought of her back as an erogenous zone, but Mac’s hands sliding over her flesh convinced her. She felt the heat build in her abdomen as his hands slid around to her ribs, drifting lightly over her heated skin. Just as his fingers brushed against the sides of her breasts, she felt a rush of moisture and a sudden tingling that seemed to beg for his hands to touch her more intimately.

Mac leaned his head forward and nibbled delicately at the skin along her shoulders.

Emily thought she would explode when he glided his hands onto her breasts and cupped their heaviness, simultaneously leaning against her. As her nipples tightened and moisture flooded her, she felt his arousal pressing into the silk at her lower back. His fingers played over her nipples, gently coaxing them to summits of pleasure.

Reciprocating, she leaned back and gently ground her hips against him. With a soft moan, Mac swung her around and held her body against the length of him. He stared down into her eyes for a few moments before he pressed his lips against her mouth.

She had barely registered their touch before he began feathering his tongue against her lips, teasing her to open to him. Her tongue met his, touching and probing the new treasure of his mouth. He seemed to urge her to deeper exploration even as he filled her mouth.

Emily pressed her body against his, wanting to be closer, regretting the clothing between them. Mac’s hands continued their exploration of her body, slipping across the naked skin of her back and up to her shoulders, sliding down her arms to her elbows and guiding her hands from his waist to lower on his body.

She traced the sculpture of his buttocks, massaging gently. But it wasn't enough. Her hands had but one destination—the fly of his trousers. His erection bucked against her hands and she quickly pushed back, pressing her belly into him in an age-old longing. He responded again, his swollen penis pushing restlessly against the fabric of his pants.

Their kiss deepened as they explored one another, standing in the doorway to Emily's living room, the police operation forgotten.

The phone's ring jolted against their passion and interrupted their kiss. By the second ring, their mouths had joined again, and their bodies pressed together, preparing for a dance of love.

The answering machine clicked on, offering to take a message. Suddenly, Angela's nervous voice filled the room.

"Emily, are you there?" She paused for a moment. "Can you pick up if you're there?"

Helplessly Mac and Emily looked at each other with regret.

"Duty calls." Emily picked up the phone. "You just caught me in time," she looked at Mac and grinned. "I don't want to be late."

"No, me either, but I've got a bit of a problem," sighed Angela.

"What's up?"

"Well, this is going to sound silly, but I don't know what to wear."

"Just like you're going out for dinner."

"I know. But how sexy should I dress? I don't want to give the wrong impression."

Emily laughed and Angela joined in. "I'd go for understated elegance. Have you got a plain black dress, some patent pumps and a pearl necklace?"

"Well, everything but the pearls. Think some really good Victorian replica jewelry would do?"

"I think you'll look just great. Just remember, wear clothes you can move in if you have to. We don't aim for you to be alone with this guy, but you need to be prepared for anything."

"Gotcha." There was a pause. "Emily, thanks for the advice."

"No problem, Angela. You'd have come up with it on your own anyway."

"I guess." There was another pause. "And thanks for the vote of confidence on putting me on this task force."

"You earned the confidence. You're an excellent cop and you're going to make an outstanding detective."

"Thanks."

"Okay, now get dressed and I'll see you at the restaurant. Good luck, Angela."

"Thanks. Let's go get us a bad guy. See ya."

Emily hung up the phone and looked across the room at Mac. He was sitting on the couch watching her. She felt suddenly shy; the distance between them looked immense. Then he held out his hand.

Walking toward him, she smiled. What was the effect this man had on her that no other ever had?

"What do you do to me, Emily, that no other woman has ever done?" Mac's voice was husky and filled with real curiosity.

The experienced detective started as she stared at him. It was as if he were reading her thoughts again. "I think it's the dress, Mac." She smiled, trying to brush off the connection.

"No, it's not. There's something about you that makes me think about forever. Come, sit beside me," he invited.

"Only for a minute. We've got to leave for the restaurant shortly."

"I know."

Emily settled beside this man she felt she'd known forever. He tugged her gently under his arm and snuggled her close against his chest. As their passion bubbled below the surface, Mac lifted her chin with one finger and turned her face up to his. "I mean it, Emily. There's something about you that goes to the core of me. Do you feel it?"

Emily stared deeply into his eyes. "I've felt it from the moment I met you. I want you physically with a passion I've never experienced before. I know your heart like my own and want to protect it from the fear you're feeling on my behalf. I want time with you, to let whatever this is between us, evolve into whatever it's meant to be. It's like I recognize you across time and space. Does that make sense?"

"Perfectly." He dipped his head and brushed his lips over hers. "I can't bear that you're putting yourself in harm's way."

"It's my job to catch this guy."

"But not at the expense of your life."

"Mac, it won't come down to that. This is a police operation that's going to be carefully monitored. Besides," she looked up at him, "Angela could draw the date with our rapist."

I can't believe I just said that.

Mac shook his head. "I don't think she will. That's not how this is meant to be. This is *your* takedown. I know it and you know it. What I really fear, is that he'll know it, too. You must be extra careful. This hunter is experienced and he's not careless."

"I'm experienced, too."

"But he knows about the dark side of humanity. He courts it and delights in it. You're out of your depth there, I fear."

"Perhaps, but I'm a cop and I know how to take care of myself."

"I know, Emily, and I'm counting on that. Still, you're dealing with someone who wants to play outside the rules. To him, the rules are made for others."

"You sound like you've met him."

"Not this particular guy, but when I covered the crime beat, I saw my share of predators. I sense this guy is more dangerous than any of those."

"Really? How so?" Emily needed to know his perspective.

"He's slicker than anyone I came across. This guy has fooled educated women into believing he's something he's not. He has built elaborate personas they believed. He's trapped them in places they felt safe. This guy takes pleasure from the game, and once you've attracted his attention, I don't think much will deter it."

"That's why I intend to stop him." She stood up and reached out her hand to him. "Come on, let's go to dinner."

* * *

Mac smiled sadly. He knew there was nothing more he could do. This chase was Emily's cause and he was lucky to be included. She could have refused his help and kept him out of the investigation. But she hadn't. Emily was the toughest, strongest woman he'd ever met. Still, he sensed a gentle creature below the surface who would sleep late with him on Saturday mornings and give him back rubs at the end of a hectic day. His grim smile relaxed.

"What are you smiling at?" she asked.

"Just thinking about you giving me a back rub."

On the way to the restaurant they chatted lightly, their shared moment of passion and connection comfortably linking them. For now, they settled into a sense of belonging together. It wasn't necessary for them to chase what was developing between them; their relationship would be consummated when the time was right.

At Breadstix, no one would ever know the effect Emily's dress had on Mac. When they followed the maitre d' to their table, the newspaper man placed his hand at the small of her back and gently guided her to a chair, then seated himself, smiling slightly and without lust, despite what the dress did to him.

This was work and he knew it. He took care of the restaurant details, ordering wine and appetizers, smoothly providing Emily the time she needed to prepare. The maitre d' pointed out Angela's table. Emily made a trip to the ladies' room reconnoitering the layout. She marked Ryan and Megan's table on the way back. She knew they'd arrive in ten minutes.

"Everything okay?" Mac asked solicitously. Anyone overhearing would just assume a concerned husband or boyfriend.

"It's great."

After pouring them each a glass of wine, Mac offered her a garlic bread stick for which the restaurant was famous. They nibbled and pretended to drink their wine as they waited for the evening to begin. They carried off their charade perfectly, looking very much the successful young professional couple out for a nice dinner. When Ryan and Megan walked past their table, they merely nodded like acquaintances from the racquet club.

A short time later, Angela arrived and was seated at the designated table. Not even by a flicker of a glance did the two couples betray their recognition of Angela.

Gord arrived a few minutes later. He and Angela chatted and laughed easily through their drinks and hors d'oeuvres. Angela's interaction with him became relaxed.

This concerned Emily.

Barbara had warned them all more than once that dropping their guard with the stalker, even momentarily, could lead to disaster. Heeding the psychologist's words, Emily watched the table carefully, even as she and Mac appeared to flirt with one another. She ate whatever he'd ordered for her without tasting it, and laughed and chatted without any idea of what they'd said. If Angela had let down her guard, it was up to Emily to be even more vigilant.

When Angela excused herself and headed to the ladies' room, Emily followed her unobtrusively. Inside, Emily quickly made certain they were alone. After settling side by side before the vanity mirror, the two women pulled out lipsticks, as if they were about to adjust their makeup.

"Angela, don't relax around this guy. What's going on?"

"Don't worry. If this is the guy, Barbara will have to retire from her profiling career."

"What do you mean?"

"Well, remember how she told us he'd be romantic and fill us with visions of moonlit walks on the beach, candlelight and talk of a perfect childhood?"

"Yeah. She said he'd be able to lay it on very convincingly."

"Well, Gord lives with his retired florist Mom and is working on a perfect hybrid geranium. It's a scented variety that will smell like a tea rose when he's done. That's one of his Mom's favorite fragrances. He's even going to name it the Priceless Priscilla for his Mom, when he gets it right. It's all we've talked about."

Angela giggled. "There hasn't been a whisper about a walk on any beach. We have, however, discussed the benefits of making compost from vegetable trimmings from his kitchen and how it compares to farm-fresh manure in the garden. We even discussed his mother's trick knee, which has really put a dent in her gardening this past season. He's a dear man looking for someone to love. He's not a serial rapist."

"You're sure?"

"He was appalled when I ordered my meat rare."

"It could be an act to throw you off."

"It could be, but remember, this guy wants to attract me, a young art dealer, not throw me off with talk of compost, sheep manure and arthritic joints."

The two women looked at each other and smiled in relief. While they wanted to catch the rapist stalking the women of Yorktown, they were human and glad for this respite.

"Hey, this was a good dry run," said Emily. "We got a chance to check out our procedure and it works. I could even read your body language."

The washroom door pushed open and the two women turned to repairing their lipstick. Megan walked in and glanced around before raising her eyebrows.

Emily nodded. "It's okay."

"Angela, Ryan wants to remind you not to relax around this scuz too much." She looked at them. "But I think I'm late on that one, aren't I?" She grinned. "Ryan was so relieved you finally came in here so I could deliver his message. He thinks your guard is down. But…you don't think he's the guy, do you?"

"No," said Emily. "And I think Angela's instincts are right on. But we were also just saying it's been a great test run for us, made even better now that we've confirmed you and Ryan are on our wavelength."

"I gotta scoot back out there," said Angela. "Don't want Gord to get anxious. He said his Mom slipped once in the bathroom and he's been nervous about that ever since." She glanced at her watch. "He wants to be home by ten to check on her. If I want dessert, I better skedaddle."

"Just to be on the safe side, Megan and Ryan will follow you home when you leave," said Emily. "Better safe than sorry. Don't go straight home. Take a roundabout route and let them see if anyone tails you."

"We know, boss." The other two laughed.

When Emily rejoined Mac, a slice of chocolate torte and a cup of espresso sat at her place; he had ordered a wedge of cheesecake and a pot of tea for himself. She noticed he'd paid the bill, leaving the receipt where she could see it. When he saw her glance at it, he picked up his fork and sampled his dessert, then casually tucked the receipt in his breast pocket.

"I can hardly wait for dessert." She slid a fork overflowing with melting chocolate ecstasy into her mouth. It was shaping up to be a wonderful evening.

* * *

Perspiration broke out along his brow as anticipation coursed through him. It was just moments before he revealed the name of the woman he'd tagged for his own.

Expertly he scanned the files, finding the one marked "ads-in." She would be there. He searched carefully, knowing she would reveal herself to him from among the many pathetic creatures.

Suddenly, there she was. He could barely contain his excitement as he read her ad.

He would stalk her with the romance she so obviously craved in her search for someone with whom to share her life. He would lure her into his snare with tales of moonlight, candlelight and starlight. He would calm her nerves with poetic talk of beaches and firesides. He laughed lightly. She would be his. The hunt had begun. He spoke her name into the silence of his lair.

"Emma Poston."

CHAPTER 8

Emily smiled at Mac as they stood up from the table. The stake out hadn't netted them their rapist. But, despite the circumstances, she'd enjoyed herself more at this dinner than at any time she could remember. Mac offered her his arm; it felt perfectly right to snuggle against him as they left the restaurant.

"You haven't seen my place." Mac glanced at her sideways. "Would you like to come over for a while?"

"I thought you'd never ask." Emily smiled at the handsome man beside her. "But I can't stay for long. I want to be in early tomorrow to go over any new ad responses we might have gotten."

"Who is picking up your mail from the box at the newspaper?" There was concern in Mac's voice.

"Don't worry. I thought about our guy watching the box and I hired an independent courier service to visit the box at the beginning of a shift and pick up the mail. If our target has a job—and he must to support the lifestyle he fronts to these successful women—he can't follow a courier all day to see where the drop-off is made at the end of a shift."

"You have done undercover work before."

"Yep. And I have a huge stake in catching this freak."

Mac unlocked the passenger door of his navy Jaguar and Emily slid onto the soft leather seat, noting the car's luxury. It was obviously new, and had an oak dash, leather interior, c-d player, sunroof. It had it all. *This beats the daylights out of my four-year-old Jeep.* And it suited

Mac's designer clothes and GQ good looks.

As they glided across town. a companionable silence drifted between them, filled only with soft jazz from the compact disc system. Mac even seemed to attract green lights. Emily smiled to herself. She'd never met anyone quite like this man. He was as real as they came, and he certainly enjoyed the good things in life.

"How old is this car?" Emily asked idly.

"I just got it about six months ago," he answered. "Do you like it?"

"What's not to like? But I'd spend all my time worrying about a scratch in the paint or a ding in a bumper."

"I did that with my first Jag. But the way I figure it is, even if I bought a minivan or a regular four-door sedan, I'd have to contend with scratches or dents. And there are so many of those models around, a dealer will nail you for every single mark when trade-in time arrives. At least with a luxury car like this, they're willing to give you a good trade because they know they'll make a mint in the used market."

"Makes sense."

"When I was thirteen, I had a paper route delivering a daily financial newspaper. I started saving for my first car then. I was thirty before I could actually buy it. So, it's really a childhood fantasy come true. One of many I worked hard to make a reality."

"What other fantasies do you have?" Emily could feel her face flush at what she'd just said.

Mac laughed. "I know what you mean." His glance flicked over to her. "Although I could share some of my more intimate fantasies with you as well."

"Stick to the childhood ones come true."

"I wanted to have a home of my own, and I do."

"That's not so unusual a dream."

"It was for us. My Mom was a single parent and we lived in some pretty ugly apartments when I was growing up. A real home was very important to me."

"I can imagine. But now you've got it. Is it what you wanted?"

"Yes and no."

"Why yes and no?"

"Well, the house is just what I wanted. It's solid stone, with fireplaces in the living room and master bedroom. There's a two-car garage and a swimming pool. It even contains a family room with a regulation pool table and home theater."

"Sounds pretty much like a perfect home." Emily sighed thinking of her three-bedroom ranch she would share with the bank until her mortgage was paid in another fifteen years.

"Oh, it's a great house, but it's not a *home*. There are no people filling it with the clutter of everyday life like laundry, dirty dishes, and half-read books on the tables. And there are no pets."

"Why?"

"Because I'd never found the person who fit the house."

Emily glanced down at her lap, suddenly filled with the knowledge she could be on some sort of trial once they arrived at Mac's. "Why don't you own a dog or a cat? Did you have a pet as a boy?"

"We had a small mixed breed we got from the local shelter. I really miss having a dog around the house."

"So why don't you get one?"

"Strange as it sounds, it seemed even more lonely, knowing a dog was waiting at the house, doing its best to fill my heart at the end of a long day. I thought it would be too much to expect of a creature I love. No, a pet fits a home, not a house." Mac swung the car into a long, interlocking stone driveway. The headlights illuminated a huge stone house with attached garage.

"Wow." It was all Emily could utter.

The rambling bungalow loomed ahead of her, big enough for a whole family. It was surrounded by perfect grass and professional landscaping, and sat in the middle of a double lot so neither next-door neighbor encroached on the occupant's privacy. Mac pushed a button on a remote control and the garage door slid up. Expertly, he guided his Jag into its parking place.

Once inside, Emily's awe grew. Obviously this house had been decorated by a designer. The kitchen was a gourmet chef's dream come true. Stainless steel appliances were placed to make food preparation easy. The counter tops were granite and a cooking island stretched across the middle of the kitchen, over which hung the most expensive pots and pans on the market. In a bow window sat an exquisite, antique oak breakfast table with a vase of fresh flowers at its center.

"Coffee okay, or would you prefer espresso?"

"Coffee would be great."

Mac ground beans and started a pot of coffee brewing. Swinging around he hooked one of the chairs out from the table. "Grab a seat while the coffee runs through."

Emily sank onto the chair and watched how comfortably Mac moved around his designer kitchen. In moments he had a tray assembled with cookies, cream and sugar, and a small decanter of brandy for the coffee. He dropped onto the chair across from her and grinned.

"Surprised you, didn't I?"

"Well, maybe a bit," she confessed with a grin. "But I like a man who knows his way around the kitchen."

"I'm a wizard with toasted English muffins and scrambled eggs on a breakfast tray," he hinted, his eyes serious.

"I love English muffins. Would there be any grape jelly for them?"

Their banter was interrupted by the sounds of the coffee pot gurgling to the end of its cycle. Mac put the pot onto the tray and turned to Emily. "How about having our coffee in the study. It's much cozier."

Emily nodded and followed him through the house. A wide hallway ran down the center of the first floor, from which Emily glimpsed other rooms as impressive as the kitchen, including a formal dining room and perfect off-white living room. They entered a room near the front door.

Emily gasped.

"Mac, it's my dream room," she managed. "It's perfect." And to her, it was.

Soft, amber-colored walls were lined with bookshelves filled with books. Artwork depicting wildlife adorned wall space not covered with the shelves. Two over-stuffed love seats and a pair of inviting wing chairs were set to take advantage of natural light for reading. The windows were covered in louvered wood shades. Mac tipped them shut to provide the pair privacy.

The room made Emily feel as if she'd found a special corner where the world could never touch her.

"I'm glad you like it. This and my bedroom were the only two rooms I didn't allow the designers from Today's Interiors to decorate. And, let me tell you, I had to battle them tooth and nail to get this the way I wanted it. Do you realize," he asked with a smile, "there are no conversation 'arenas' in this room?"

"I noticed immediately," Emily said in a mockingly stern voice. "How do you suppose it is we're actually able to talk in here?"

"Somehow, we've managed." They grinned at one another.

Mac continued, "This room is for me to sit and read my papers and books, and just to think. It's not for entertaining." Mac set down the tray on the low oval coffee table in front of the nearest love seat.

Emily felt a thrill of joy shimmer through her. Mac had brought her to the part of the house that truly embodied him. She smiled as the happiness that had quivered around her all evening slid home into her heart.

"If you're saying that so you don't have to pour me a cup of coffee, you're sadly mistaken, my dear editor friend."

"I'd be honored to pour you coffee, my delightful undercover police detective."

They sat on the love seat, and he offered her a dollop of brandy for her coffee. Emily nodded, saying, "You're not having any?"

"Well, I might be driving you home later."

"Hhmmm." Emily hadn't decided yet whether she should stay with him or not. Her every instinct told her this man was the one for whom she'd unconsciously been searching. But her common sense told her she hadn't known him long enough to be spending the night with him. Should their first sexual encounter be at her home, where she felt most in control?

As if they'd been together for years instead of days, their conversation swirled easily as they talked about the news of the day. The minutes flew by as they discussed their favorite authors and foods, vacation spots and pet peeves. They decided they were never going to agree on what books would be on their shelves, but both were inveterate readers. Mac leaned toward the Tom Clancy and Robert Ludlum massive thrill-tomes, while Emily much preferred sinking her teeth into a Martha Grimes mystery or reveling in an Olivia Goldsmith slap at conventions. She admitted to him that her favorite best-selling author had started out writing romances; she'd read every one of them, and loved them.

Emily's dream vacation plans revolved around long hikes up mountains; Mac thought stretching out on a beach without a cell phone was the perfect getaway. They acknowledged not being able to remember the last time they'd actually taken a vacation.

"I spent two weeks last summer repainting my parents' cottage up north," admitted Emily. "But I did get in some hiking during the mosquito hours just before sundown each day."

"Well, the last time I was actually on a beach, I was covering a story on an oil slick off the west coast."

As their conversation meandered, they shared their dreams and fears, discovering areas of similarity and great differences. Their contentment grew in the cozy warmth of the study.

Mac refilled their mugs. Emily had just decided she'd stay the night, and had picked up the decanter to pour brandy into both mugs when Mac's pager shrilled. They looked at each other before she nodded and he checked the number.

"Sorry, it's the press room. Do you mind if I take this?"

"No, Mac, go ahead."

He picked up the phone and hit a speed dial number. In moments he was talking to the press boss. Emily could tell how important it was by Mac's tone of voice. By the time he was off the phone, she had the coffee remains stacked on the tray.

"I'm sorry."

"Don't worry. If anyone understands, I do."

"It's the morning edition. There's a problem with one of the pages. I'm going to have to revise the whole layout as quickly as possible to get the press running again."

"An editor's life, eh?"

"I'd still like it if you'd stay. I'll only be gone for an hour or so."

Emily glanced at her watch. "It'd be great, but I promised myself I'd be in by seven tomorrow morning. If you don't mind dropping me at my house on the way downtown?"

"Sure." The disappointment was heavy in his voice. "Damn this thing anyway."

"Mac," Emily reached out and laid her hand on his arm. "The next time we're together, I'll plan to spend the night with you."

He looked quickly at her and she heard his breath hiss in. "Are you sure?"

"I'm sure. Very sure indeed."

She slid into his arms and pressed herself against the length of him. She could feel the strength of his body against her. His immediate response to her closeness bumped strongly against her belly. Heat poured from her center and filled her. Emily was conscious of her nipples hardening under the silk of her dress and pebbling tautly against his chest.

She stretched up and pressed her lips against his, tracing their pattern with her tongue before she allowed herself to explore his mouth. Mac responded immediately, his hands caressing her naked back, wandering under the edges of her dress. Emily's eyes slid shut as she released herself to the sensation of kissing Mac thoroughly.

His hands trailed across her skin and onto her buttocks pulling her closer against him. His erection pressed firmly against her and Emily felt her passion answer his. Being with Mac would be wonderful. Her heart told her he would be an inventive but gentle lover.

Their breath mingling, they ended the kiss, not wanting to torment themselves any longer.

"At least we have time to get blood tests done," Mac said, smiling lovingly at her.

"Then no worries about being together."

Emily felt a small prickle of regret as she slid into the front seat of the Jaguar and looked at the handsome man climbing into the driver's seat. Mac turned to her, and their eyes met. They leaned toward one another for an intimate kiss.

Emily felt her nipples peak again, betraying her to his touch as Mac's finger tips stroked her breast. Without a word, the caress ended and Mac started the car. The time seemed to fly past as they drove through town, Mac's hand resting on her thigh.

The pair walked to her front door. Mac waited while she unlocked the door. He kissed her deeply once more, and they reveled in the passion they aroused in each other. Too soon, their evening had ended, but it glittered brightly with the promise of their next time together.

* * *

He held his breath as he squirted Sunflowers perfume onto the response he'd crafted so carefully. His sensitive nostrils had picked up her fragrance in the elevator. It hadn't taken him long to pick it out at the cosmetics counter. It was his special touch, designed to lure her closer. She'd feel safer if he was masked in her scent.

Eyes narrowing, he tipped back the beer and swallowed deeply as he read his response to her signal. It was designed to disarm her, attract her to him. He'd put his whole being into writing it.

His tongue raced hungrily over his teeth. He had to get this into her mail slot at the newspaper tonight.

He felt his need for her rise, stronger than ever.

Carefully, he slid the letter into the envelope and licked ravenously at the glue. Then he nestled it into his jacket breast pocket, shut out the lights and exited his office in total darkness.

CHAPTER 9

By the time Mac had fixed the layout, he was wired and not ready to go home. He decided to stop by his office and check his e-mail. As he rode up in the elevator, he smiled as he thought about Emily and the love she'd brought into his life so quickly. He'd thought himself completely immersed in his successful career, but from the moment she'd entered his office, he'd been entranced by her. Emily was a unique blend of tough cop and sexy lady. He found it impossible to categorize her. Mac readily acknowledged the depth of his new feelings, even as he accepted how quickly they'd overwhelmed him and how unusual that was for him.

Stepping off the elevator, Mac swung his head quickly to the right. He thought he'd seen something move in the classifieds department. Nothing. He waited for a moment, hoping whatever had attracted his attention would catch it once more. Still nothing.

Shaking his head, he entered his office, letting his thoughts drift back to the evening with Emily. Guided by ambient light from the main office, he crossed to his desk and flicked on the lamp. As he powered up his computer, he looked at the couch where he'd first encountered Emily.

If she'd only known my thoughts, even then.

She'd radiated a healthy sexiness without seeming to be aware of it, or her effect on him. Mac remembered how hard it had been to concentrate when all he'd wanted to do was run his fingers through the wavy curls tumbling around her shoulders. How he'd ached to feather his fingers over the soft skin of her cheek, to stroke the little hollow at the base of her neck and feel her pulse race in response to his touch.

The beep of his computer brought him back to reality. Mac punched in his personal passwords and quickly scanned the electronic messages. Realizing all of them could wait until morning, he decided he was unwound enough to pack it in for the night. His day had been jammed full of meetings, including one with his department heads that had put him behind schedule for the rest of the day.

He'd had to hurry to meet Emily at the proscribed time for their dinner. But it had been worth the rush. He could still feel the sensuous combination of silk and skin he'd explored before dinner. As his hands had teased between flesh and fabric, he'd been as excited as Emily. He could hardly wait for the time when they could be together. His mind wandered to tantalizing thoughts of making love to her.

He crossed the main office, automatically glancing around, checking that everything was all right. Once again the sensation of movement tugged at his unconscious and he paused, every sense alert. His eyes roved over the desks and chairs scattered around the room. There was no one at work, but the lights were on in the kitchen. He grinned. That's what had caught his eye—a shadow cast by an unexpected light source. He trotted across the room and clicked off the light, then headed back to the elevator. He pushed the button, and in moments a car slid open in front of him. Yawning and stretching his arms widely, Mac stepped into the elevator.

* * *

His mouth tightened in a grimace as he watched Mac leave. How easily he could have stalked the editor in the dark, savaged him and left the body for the morning staff to find. He smiled as he thought of Mac's blood-stained, destroyed form being discovered by his secretary. The resulting hysteria would have been thrilling. And how he could have pretended to share the outrage and the shock, all the while reveling in his kill!

But that would have ended the more important game. Police would have flooded the newspaper office, and everything would have come to a halt. He would have had to postpone his pursuit of Emma during the investigation.

More than anything, he wanted to capture Emma and have her for his own. It was the only reason Mac was still alive.

He felt his bloodlust simmer to life as he thought about his delectable Emma. How much sport she would provide him. With her lithe, athletic build she'd be a physical challenge, but he would force her to his will and she would become his. She would be the one to stay with him a while, he decided. But this new game involved risks. Because in holding her, she would get to know about him. And then Emma could become dangerous. He had no intention of becoming the stalked rather than the stalker.

The blood pounded through his veins and he snarled silently in the dark. Without a sound, he walked to the bank of mail slots and crammed his perfectly-crafted reply to Emma into her mailbox. He had no doubt he would hear from her shortly.

CHAPTER 10

Emily arrived at the precinct by seven o'clock the next morning. Within minutes, she'd covered the boardroom table with notes conveying new information her task force had accumulated. She shook her head. Their target chose his victims carefully and had matched himself to their romantic fantasies perfectly. There was no doubt in Emily's mind that if she was going to stop the hunter-at-large in Yorkton, she would have to pretend to fall under his spell; to be completely captivated by his act. Anything less would result in failure and that was unacceptable.

He must be stopped. No matter what the cost.

Thoughts swirling, she walked to the coffee machine and poured her third cup of the morning. It was going to be a long day, no doubt about it. With a sigh, she returned to the boardroom. There, bent over the table, Angela shuffled through a file. She looked up as Emily entered the room.

"Good morning, Emily," the younger officer greeted her with a warm smile. "Last night wasn't exactly what we expected, was it?"

"No, it wasn't. You know, you did a great job, Angela. Your street experience sure paid off, reading Gord so perfectly. I'm glad you're with us."

"Thanks, Emily. I wanted to do a great job. But, it going to the *team* that takes him down."

Just then Ryan and Barbara arrived, talking as they entered the room. Barbara dropped a few envelopes onto the table. "Not much mail yet today."

"The courier service will deliver again around noon," said Emily. "We should have a few more responses to go over this afternoon."

"I was really worried last night," stated Ryan baldly. "I don't want this rapist to get past us somehow."

"No chance of that ever happening," replied Angela.

They spent the rest of the morning going over the material they'd amassed. Barbara identified a few more characteristics about their suspect. She told them he would be meticulous, exacting and probably extremely physically fit. It was a frightening picture she painted very clearly.

"I want to remind everyone, including myself, that he pictures himself a hunter and feels superior to his prey. We cannot let down our guard for even a moment with any of our suspects," said Emily seriously. "This guy could be anyone. He has been successful so far because he blends in so well.

"He is an expert at hiding in the open, camouflage in place, so his victim won't recognize him even when he stands in front of her. And one of us will be walking willingly into his trap." She looked around the room. "He will not hesitate to make the kill. We must always remember it, even when we're face to face with his charm. Or," she hesitated and glanced at Angela, "it could prove tragic. And deadly."

* * *

By noon, they had agreed the next date would be Emily's. Unless something was booked sooner, the scheduled engagement would be Emily's lunch the following Monday. Ryan and Angela would serve as backup. Mac would be left out. She knew the newspaper man would not be happy about it, but Emily recognized that this engagement was hers to play out. Mac had no role in it, and wouldn't until the next time Angela dined with a suspect. Then, Mac could join Emily as back up, once again.

Having organized Emily's luncheon, the group focused on identifying a partner to have dinner with her before her Tuesday evening with Jonas. While they'd identified three potential suspects, they decided to wait for the noon mail delivery from the newspaper to make a final choice.

Just as they were about to break for lunch, the phone rang. Emily answered, somehow knowing it was Mac. She was not looking forward to this conversation. Mac would not be pleased that he'd been removed from the next stake out.

"Might as well get it over with," she muttered as she picked up the phone.

"Hey there," said Mac.

"Hey there yourself."

"I'm really sorry about our interruption last night. If it hadn't been an emergency, the evening would certainly have ended differently…I hope." There was just a suggestion of a leer in his voice.

"I agree. Emergencies always happen at a most inconvenient time, don't you think?" She found herself smiling. Mac had that effect on her.

"Meet me for lunch." His voice was husky. "I need to see you."

Emily's pulse pounded like a runaway stagecoach team. "How about the Overtime Diner at the corner of Maple and Dundas in fifteen minutes?"

"See you there." With a click he was gone.

Emily grabbed her jacket and left the precinct. Within minutes she was at the tiny restaurant. Mac was already seated in a booth. He waved to her, and she grinned as she slid in across from him.

"Setting up the next date? Got any candidates yet?" Mac looked at her carefully.

"Just a few. More mail came in already today, but we're waiting until the courier delivery after lunch to make the final call on who I go out with." Emily let the silence grow for a few seconds. "I need to talk to you about that date."

"What do you mean?" Mac's voice was full of suspicion. "I thought we had already discussed this."

"Yes, we have. But I'm not sure you're totally clear on everything." She reached across the table and covered his clenched fist with her hand. "This is still a police matter and your participation, while appreciated, must remain that of a civilian. Your safety is paramount."

"So is yours, Emily. This sicko is planning to attack another woman. I don't want her to be you." He leaned forward, his eyes lasering into hers.

Just as Emily was about to answer, the waitress appeared with a coffee pot in one hand and menus in the other. "Today's soup is split pea and our lunch special is a toasted western with fries." She dropped menus in front of each of them. "Coffee?" She held up the pot, and when they both nodded, she filled their crockery mugs and deposited a handful of creamers on the table. "Be back in a jiff." She spun away to answer the sharp ping of the pick-up bell from the kitchen.

Emily delayed the conversation by swirling cream and sugar into her mug and sipping the hot coffee. "I don't particularly want to be his next victim, either. But, just as you say, this animal is planning to attack someone else.

"According to our psychologist's profile, this man is highly intelligent, amoral and feels himself superior to others, especially women. He's been very successful so far. No one has been able to stop him. He's convinced no one even knows what he is up to in Yorkton. And, feeling safe, he's tiring of the old game.

"Barbara believes, and I agree with her, that this is going to make him want to push the envelope. Up the ante in his contest, so to speak, and move into a whole new realm, even for him. Mac, we believe he's in the process of choosing someone to hold captive for a few days. And we both know what that means. That unfortunate woman won't walk away and file a police report as the other victims have been able to do."

"Emily," Mac's voice was on the edge of panic. "Do I understand you correctly? This man is planning to become a killer?"

"Are you ready to order, folks?"

Emily shot Mac a warning glance and turned to the menu. "How about a bowl of today's soup and a piece of apple pie."

The woman jotted down Emily's order and glanced at Mac.

"A hamburger deluxe with extra tomatoes. Well-done, please."

Another quick notation, a gathering of menus and their waitress disappeared.

"Okay, let's continue," said Mac. "You've told me this guy doesn't leave behind physical evidence. If he kidnaps a victim and keeps her, there's certainly going to be plenty of evidence this time. Physical and otherwise."

"You've got that right, Mac. She'll hear his voice, observe his habits, and there's absolutely no way he'll avoid DNA crossover with this sustained contact. He will leave plenty of evidence. Because he knows that, we believe that unfortunately, he will also leave a body in his wake. It's the only way he has to destroy as much evidence as possible. Forensics may be able to pick up some clues, but there'll be no talking witness to pinpoint his lair."

"And you plan to put yourself in this man's way?" Mac's voice was filled with pain.

Emily realized he'd known the answer before he'd even asked the question. "Yes, Mac," she answered quietly. "I'm hoping mine is the most attractive ad he finds among your newspaper's personals. I want him to focus on me rather than someone else in Yorkton. Because I will stop him, right in his tracks." Emily's voice was filled with determination. "Please understand, Mac."

"I understand, I really do. But just think about this. Even though we've known each other only a short time, I have feelings for you that I want time to explore. So, as I've said before, I don't want to see you in harm's way and I'm very grateful to be another pair of eyes to help protect you."

"Then you're going to be upset by what I'm about to say. You can't come on the next stake out."

"You're not saying what I think you're saying!"

"I'll be dating the next suspect, and Angela and Ryan will be my backup."

"You said I could help."

"I know I did, and you will again if this isn't the guy, but for this time, we've got everyone we need."

"What about Ryan's dinner partner from the other night?"

"Megan is another officer who is volunteering in her off time. She's on duty tomorrow when we plan to set up the next date. So Ryan goes with Angela. That leaves you out." She looked straight at him. "I'm sorry, Mac, but that's just how it is."

"I didn't interfere before and I won't this time, either. Look, I know you're highly capable, but it makes me feel better to be there, to see you're okay for myself. I hope you understand that and don't feel I lack confidence in your ability to do your job anymore than you lack confidence in my competence."

"I do understand, Mac. And you'll be my escort any time Angela is the target and Megan is working with Ryan. Look, I know your reputation….that you've worked with street cops and detectives. You give us a unique perspective, especially since we're now convinced he's stalking women through your newspaper's personal ads."

"That bastard." There was cold hatred in Mac's response. "I deserve to be in on bringing him down, you know that." He paused and took a deep breath. "But I respect what you say. I'll be ready for the next time you want me involved."

"Thanks for understanding, Mac. The time we've spent together over the past few days has meant a great deal to me. I feel like I've known you for years, not days. And I'm definitely looking forward to the time we can spend together without searching for some psychotic rapist.

"Last night was the best time I've had since...I can't remember when." Emily glanced around but there was no one close enough to overhear. "I really wish that layout emergency hadn't happened. I was so enjoying our time alone together and wanted it to last much longer." She paused for a moment. "And become much more intimate." She heard Mac's breathing accelerate immediately. "I've never met a man like you. You take my breath away, do you know that, Mac?"

"I kind of get that idea." He reached across the table and stroked her cheek with his forefinger.

"I need to go now. The task force is getting together after lunch to review the new batch of responses. Guess I'll carry out my soup."

* * *

Mac sat for a few minutes after Emily left, staring at the door she'd exited. A sudden thought jolted through him like a laser. He was in love with Emily Evans. And he was watching her set herself up as bait for someone about to kill for kicks.

He slammed his hand against the table. When the waitress looked over startled, he just shrugged and shook his head. She smiled. She'd probably seen men in love with stubborn women many times before.

* * *

Emily arrived at the boardroom before anyone else had returned from lunch. She set down her take-out lunch and the first coffee of the afternoon and sank into a chair. She didn't feel good about how she'd had to hurt Mac. She sipped coffee, allowing her thoughts to turn to the newspaper editor.

He was the strongest man she'd ever met—disciplined and dedicated to his job, but with a sense of family she found beguiling. His eyes were endlessly filled with whatever emotion he was feeling at the moment. She remembered them darkening in the privacy of his study last night after dinner.

She closed her eyes and relived the feeling of his hands drifting over her body so intimately. No man had ever made her feel the way Mac did. And no man had ever respected her professional ability the way he did.

Her hand jerked as a thought struck her and she spilled coffee across the desk. She was in love with the man, no doubt about it. Even though she'd known him for less than a week, she was in love with him. And about to risk any future they might have by setting herself up as bait for a sadistic rapist.

* * *

He looked around the office. No one was paying attention to him. He had a moment to check his prey's ad box. All the mail was gone.

Blood pound in his veins.

Today, she would read his note. His words would begin the trail that would lead her to his lair. He licked ravenously at his lips in anticipation. Oh, he would enjoy this one so much more, and so many more times than the others.

He felt a faint prick of regret for her fate, then bludgeoned it down with his lust for the hunt. She wasn't a person. She was his target.

Today, perhaps tonight alone in her home, as she read and re-read his romantic words, she'd begin to fall in love with the persona he'd designed. His decoy, the ad response, would bring him within striking distance, then it would be too late for the auburn-haired beauty he craved.

He couldn't stop the smile curving his lips as he returned to his desk.

CHAPTER 11

Emily was mopping up spilled coffee when Barbara returned.

"Have a little accident, perhaps thinking about the danger you could be facing?" Barbara's expression was wry, but her tone was sincere. She'd known the detective for years, and Emily knew the psychologist considered her strong, but not invincible.

"Well, to be honest, I just experienced an incredible revelation that startled me totally."

"A revelation, huh. Anything you'd care to share?"

"Not just yet." Emily stopped cleaning the mess, looked up at her friend and colleague, and let the grin spread across her face.

"You've fallen in love with him, haven't you?"

"Is it that obvious?"

"Well," Barbara pretended to consider for a moment. "Let me put my best psychologist's powers to work on this. You're sitting in a room with a desk covered in files from a case you're working on. Not one of those files is open, but you're grinning from ear to ear over a spilled cup of coffee. Hhhmm, what could be going on?" She opened her eyes wide and held up an index finger. "I know. You've either taken leave of your senses or you're in love with that newspaper editor you keep talking to."

Emily's smile burbled over into laughter as she hugged her friend. "It just now occurred to me what was going on. I haven't known him very long so it kind of caught me by surprise."

"Oh, I see. You have to know someone a set amount of time before your heart can recognize love?"

"Yes, I always thought so. I really did. It never crossed my mind it could happen in a flash. I believed everyone who touted love at first sight was really talking about lust at first sight."

Emily paused for a moment, then rushed on before she lost her courage to talk about her feelings for Mac. "Not that there isn't lust, but it's so much more between us. He looks at me and I feel like he's touching me. He touches me and I want to spend forever in his bed. But it's not just that. He has a house he's really trying to make a home. He's intelligent, focused, family-oriented, handsome and so good at his job. He's pushed hard to get where he is. He worked the crime beat for years. He knows cops and how important our jobs are to us."

Emily stopped abruptly. "I'm blathering."

Barbara smiled. "You know I've been married to Tom for nearly thirty years. We have three grown children and two grandchildren, and we still plan romantic weekends for two. So I do understand. You're not blathering, Emily. You're in love. Have you ever stopped to listen to how often I talk about Tom, even after all these years? And I use practically the same words you just did."

"Mac is the first man I've met in a long time who talks to me—not at me or down to me—just to me. I could talk to him forever. Granted," Emily grinned again before she said, "I do admit, I'd like to spend that talking time with the two of us naked."

The two women were still laughing when Angela and Ryan returned from lunch. Once Emily had refilled her mug and everyone was settled around the table, they started on the stack of mail the courier had picked up that morning. Eight envelopes—five of them had canceled stamps, the other three had been dropped off at the newspaper.

Ryan pointed to the three envelopes. "No telling if anyone even remembers these arriving."

"They could have arrived overnight through the newspaper's drop slot," Angela reminded them. "Whoever picked up the stack of mail this morning would've distributed everything to where it belonged—desks, post office boxes or classifieds."

"Well, let's hope our guy is lurking in one of these responses," said Emily as she donned latex gloves and picked up the plain white envelope on top of the pile. "'I'm the answer to your dreams. Let me make all your dreams come true,'" she read aloud from the blue paper. "Whew! This guy dosed this stationery with his cologne."

Angela picked it up and sniffed. "Yuck. I think his cat peed on it."

Laughter erupted as the tension released momentarily.

Barbara perused the letter and passed it on to Ryan. "What does everyone think?"

"It's not him," stated Emily emphatically.

"I agree." Ryan and Angela chorused together.

"Why's that?" asked Barbara, looking at Emily.

"I don't think our rapist will be this gentle and soft. There's certainly a control component to this guy's personality with his arrogance of letting *him* make her dreams come true. But he's not catering to her romantic side."

"That's right." Angela jumped in. "This one reads a lot of mushy cards, but I don't think he's an original enough thinker to be our guy. The stalker wants to lure her in, capture her imagination."

"Open another," said Ryan. "The cologne guy isn't going out on a date with either of you."

It took them the better part of an hour to work through the pile of responses. Each person took a turn opening and reading the contents to the others in the room. Emily's coffee cooled until it became undrinkable. With only two more letters to open, they decided to take a break and stretch their minds and legs for a few minutes.

Emily touched Barbara's arm on her way by. "Please don't mention what we talked about earlier. I was just overwhelmed by my…discovery. I've never felt like this before."

"Don't worry, sweetie, your secret's safe with me 'til you're ready to reveal all." She patted Emily on the shoulder. "Now, I'm going to put on the kettle and make a cup of tea before we tackle these last two letters."

Within fifteen minutes everyone had reassembled.

Emily knew the moment her gloved fingers touched the envelope that this was what they'd been waiting for. She couldn't say why, but she knew when she opened it, she'd have him in her sights. Carefully she slit the envelope and pulled out the sheet of heavy, cream-colored stationery.

She unfolded it and took a deep breath.

"'The moonlight-dappled water washes warmly over our sandy feet as we wander the night beach sharing memories and making new ones. If you'd like to share remembrances and create tomorrow's memories together, I'd love to start with dinner. Please call and let me know where we can share a meal together.' It's signed, 'Andrew Morrison.'"

Emily looked around the room. "It's him."

"Let's analyze what we've got," cautioned Barbara. "What makes you so sure this guy is him?"

"He's touched on everything—memory, moonlight, the romance of walking on a beach, the gentle approach pretending to give her control. That would certainly feed his fantasy. He'll let her think she's safe while he's really baiting a trap for her. I think he gets off on that. You know, the superiority of knowing the ultimate end to the relationship. It doesn't work if she's skittish. He only gets what he wants if she feels totally relaxed with him. If she trusts him."

"He could just be a really romantic guy," offered Angela. "But there aren't many of them around. Gotta admit, his act is good though. I'd love to walk on a moonlit beach as the warm waves flow over my feet. Of course, along with the fantasy, I'm wearing a designer gown, I look like Sharon Stone, and my Porsche is waiting in the parking lot."

They all laughed.

"But look how his letter has you thinking," said Barbara.

"We want to buy the fantasy," added Emily. "There are no dead fish on this beach, no homeless people looking for coins. With him, it's just moonlight and romance. This is our guy." She was emphatic.

"So, you want to go out with him?" asked Ryan. "Nail his sadistic butt to a prison wall?"

"You got it. We'll get an answer back to him. And let's dust this letter for prints. Maybe we'll get lucky and get a match from somewhere else. He didn't just spring full-blown into the area without having a history of rape. Maybe somebody got prints from something else he's done."

Ryan was able to lift a partial thumb print from one corner and a blurred fingerprint from the fold line. While he worked, the three women composed a reply for Emily so she could practice reciting it. By the time she called their suspect, she didn't want to sound as if she was reading lines.

"How about this?" Emily asked. "'Hi, Andrew. This is Emma Poston and I'm calling about your answer to my ad in the personals. I love moonlight and I love beaches and I'd love to have dinner with you. One of my favorite restaurants is Breadstix. It's downtown in the theater district. Why don't I make a reservation for Friday night at seven? If Friday isn't good, just call. My number is 555-3928. Otherwise, I'll see you at seven tomorrow night. Bye. Oh, yeah, you should know that the reservation will be in my name so the maitre d' can show you to the table in case you get there first. See ya.'"

"Interested and assertive, but not off-putting. Sounds great, Emily," said Ryan.

"Agreed," responded Angela. "Just enough strength to give him a hard-on about control, but not so much he thinks you're an iron lady." She turned to the psychologist. "What do you think, Barbara?"

Barbara looked at the three officers facing her around the table. "I think you've got him lined up. The response will play to his need to let her think she's running the show while he plans his total control of her body and mind. This is the real deal, guys. It's time to be smart, careful and stay alive. This one won't hesitate to kill—not even a police officer."

A knock at the boardroom door interrupted their discussion. A lab tech stood in the doorway holding the original letter Ryan had dusted for fingerprints.

"Sorry, but there were no hits on the two prints you got. But they weren't the best prints, so he may still have a record somewhere." He handed back the letter, protected in a plastic evidence bag, and disappeared.

"It's still going to be important to have these prints in case we need to match them with those from a crime scene," said Emily. Silence descended on the room as everyone digested her meaning.

"No way will we let this sicko take you, Emily."

"He will be dead before he hits the ground," echoed Angela.

"If we don't get him one way, we'll get him another," said Emily. "Ultimately, these prints will be valuable to the investigation. Put the letter in safekeeping." She looked around the room. "Let's go over our strategy for tomorrow night."

By the end of their shift, they had their plan mapped out and were confident Emily was going to be well protected. She'd take a cab to the restaurant so Andrew couldn't track her by her car or license plate. Her purse would never leave her sight so he couldn't find out her home address. She'd have a set of business cards identifying her as an architect with a police safe house listed as her address and a very real phone number that would be electronically monitored 24 hours a day.

Angela and Ryan would be at Breadstix by seven o'clock with a clear sight line to the rendezvous point—the same table Angela had shared with Gord. Emily would arrive at the restaurant around seven-fifteen, so she'd be in place when Andrew arrived.

"Don't leave the table once he sits down, even if you feel like your bladder will burst," warned Barbara. "I imagine this guy will be a walking pharmacy. I don't want him tainting your food or drink to impair you mentally or physically."

Emily nodded. She would act cool and standoffish at first, but allow herself to thaw slightly through the meal. She'd pretend to relax slowly, listening to warm stories of an idyllic childhood that Barbara assured them he would spin.

"He won't be able to help himself," she explained. "It's part of the ritual to him. You'll hear a lot about his doting parents, family vacations and plenty of privilege. He's probably almost come to believe these tales."

Once dinner was over, they agreed Emily would not go anywhere else with Andrew, even if he insisted or pouted. She would not play hard to get she would just, with regret, plead an important business appointment early on Saturday morning for which she had to be wide awake and alert. She'd offer another date if he seemed interested. And she'd leave by police car disguised as a cab, while Angela and Ryan attempted to get the license plate number from his car. If he took a cab, too, they'd follow it to his home.

Emily needed to play the dangerous game very carefully. Andrew had to be intrigued and teased along to set the hook in him. But Barbara advised he would probably be the perfect gentleman and neither insist nor persist at this stage. He would likely send flowers to her business card address the next day and phone to thank her for the date. And, most importantly, to ask her on a second date.

"Should I wait by the phone on Saturday or set up a machine?" asked Emily.

"I really don't think he'll be upset if he gets a machine as long as you call back within an hour or so. He'll be expecting you to hope he'll call. He'll also expect you'll be dying to go out with him. Play along and let him believe you're totally fascinated by him. Be glad to hear from him. Agree to meet with him in a public place for another date."

Barbara sighed. "If this guy put his mental abilities into something positive, he'd make a real name for himself. But he prefers the hunt. So don't forget for even a second that he's hunting you, Emily. He sees you as a victim, his quarry, his prize. And, once he has you, he believes he has the right to do to you anything he wishes."

"But it won't get to that point," Emily said. "Because he'll slowly drop his guard when he thinks he has me in his grasp. And that's when he'll walk blindly into our trap."

Ryan nodded. "He won't know what hit him...that he's the one who's being snared. Don't worry, Emily. None of us will let our guards down for a moment now this has started."

"Not a moment," reiterated Angela with feeling. "He's attacked his last victim, raped his last woman. It's goodbye to whatever his real name is."

* * *

He felt like the day would never end. She had his message by now and she would read it shortly. His thoughts tumbled in anticipation. She would be intrigued by the moonlight beach, he knew. What woman wouldn't be? And the gentle approach would keep her guard from going up very far

Water washing warmly over her bare feet! He snorted at the image. Maybe when he was done with her he'd dump her body in the lake. See how much she enjoyed *that* trip to the beach.

His heart pounded madly. He'd meet her for a boring dinner date at some lame restaurant, but this time there'd be no going back. He would take her that night. No need to court this one like the others and set up the perfect alibi. He didn't care if she knew who had her. It wasn't like she'd be able to identify him to the police later.

He glanced at the receipt from the hardware store. Everything he'd ordered would be delivered today. He would soundproof his den that night. Perhaps, while he kept her in that den, he'd show her his memories and trophies. He chuckled low in his throat as he slid the receipt into a desk drawer. The memories he'd make with Emma would last her lifetime.

"Jack, do you have a moment?" A voice called from across the room.

He jerked back to reality and smiled quickly. "Sure thing, Mac. I'll be right there."

CHAPTER 12

Mac was flipping open a folder on his desk when Jack entered. "Come on in and grab a seat," he offered as he waved to a chair across the desk. "I'm just grabbing some stats to go over with you."

"You're not happy with our department?" Jack's question was underlined with aggression. "If you check it out, we're up over the last two quarters. There's no reason to be less than pleased with us."

"Quite the contrary." Mac forced a smile. "I actually want to refer to the personals section at the next editorial meeting to show other department supervisors how well it's doing." He paused, still searching through the file, then pulled out a sheaf of papers. "Here it is, Jack."

He separated a single piece of paper and perused it for a moment. Then he held it out to the man sitting across the desk from him. It had occurred to Mac that Jack was a reasonable candidate for the serial rapist. After all, the man had access to the personals on a daily basis, and was the right height and build as the police suspect. Mac planned to push him just a little and see how Jack responded. Maybe their target was closer than anyone thought.

Jack took the page, looking at it suspiciously. "What's this?"

"It's the statistics on how the personals have increased over the last few months. Can you give any reasons why?" Mac's voice was light, but his eyes studied Jack relentlessly.

"I'd say some of the promos we ran helped."

"Like the one of Amanda's offering a boxed ad for the price of a classified ad? She put some effort into making that work, don't you think?"

Jack's tone was dismissive. "That's not how to make money in a department. She'd know that if she had bothered to think it through properly." He stopped, as if catching himself and glanced up at Mac who was regarding him mildly. Jack's voice softened. "She tried hard to come up with something. But the one receiving the most response was where advertisers got an extra week if they didn't get a date from the first ad.

"And the week's subscription for the week their ad ran worked to increase circulation, too. The *Daily Gazette* is kind of known as a news stand paper and this idea of mine helped get it into more morning mail boxes. Although I don't know how many exactly."

"Four point two percent more to be exact, Jack. And about two percent of those ended up buying a yearly subscription. It was a good program. Think those ideas would work in the rest of the classified department?"

"I can't see why not."

Mac watched his employee relax, guessing that Jack believed he was leading his boss along a path he'd designed.

"If it was cross-promoted on radio and TV, and by staff when people call in, I'll bet it could work," Jack continued. "You know… If you don't sell that used crib in the week's worth of ads you buy, we give you another whole week. It would be like a money back guarantee I'll bet lots of people couldn't resist, and revenues would rise significantly. "

"You're right, Jack. I think it's worth a try, too." Mac looked at him. "Before you go, I've got something else to discuss with you, if you've got a moment." Mac kept his voice neutral and leaned forward to confide in him. "An editor friend of mine at the *Detroit Free Press* has a contact at a California paper who has had some problems with their personal ads."

"Problems?" Jack's voice was too neutral to Mac's ear. "Like what?"

Mac scrutinized the man across the desk from him. Perhaps Jack would reveal a clue if he was indeed involved in the serial rapes. "Well, it seems that some nutcase"—Mac slightly emphasized the last word—"placed an ad that lured a couple of women to a remote location and they were attacked by him. Both survived, but he'd used the personals to locate them and he stalked them from there."

"And what does that have to do with us?" Jack's eyes bored into

Mac's across the desk, challenging him.

Mac looked back, carefully hiding his scrutiny. "I just wondered if there was any way such a thing could happen with the *Daily Gazette.*"

"I supposed it could. We don't personally know everyone placing an ad. Certainly we couldn't be held responsible for someone else's action."

"Oh, no one suggested the *Free Press* was responsible. I'd just like to be sure our paper couldn't be used in such a way. Do we have any repeat advertisers that you know of, Jack?"

* * *

"Sure, lots of people place ads more than once. That's not a crime. It just means that advertising in the *Daily Gazette* works. And that's what we want after all, isn't it?" He smiled disarmingly. *If this idiot only knew how I've used the personals.*

"You're right. Of course we want our ads to work so people are return customers." Mac grinned. "I'm just being paranoid, I guess. All the years it took me to work my way to editor, I don't want to end up pounding a reporter beat again."

Jack smiled back coolly. "I can imagine."

Just then the phone shrilled. "Excuse me, Jack, it must be important. I asked that my calls be held." Mac picked up the handset. "Mac Landon here." He smiled involuntarily and his voice deepened slightly.

Jack's interest perked up immediately. His boss must be on the phone with a woman he cared about. His senses went into overtime as he eavesdropped, at the same time reflecting on his last few minutes' conversation with Mac.

Landon had been nosing around in his department, damn him. Jack felt the anger he'd pushed down at his boss' questions flow through him. Forget the phony praise about how well his section was doing.

How dare he question whether anyone would use the paper as a stalking ground. That territory belonged to Jack and no one else.

He listened carefully to Mac's end of the conversation while he pretended to go over the departmental statistics.

"Emily, I'm in a meeting. May I call you back?" He paused. "Tonight? I'm so sorry, but I have a meeting with the publisher. Every editor is expected to attend. It's one of those stand and deliver deals." He smiled across the desk at Jack and signaled he'd only be a moment. "In fact, Jack and I were just going over some—" He paused, listening without interruption. "No, I need to get all the statistics and facts about the department for tonight's meeting so I'll be a little while longer."

Another pause. "I know that very well."

The intimate tone in his voice deepened and Jack's interest piqued. "May I call you later about this? Maybe we can get together tomorrow. Okay, I understand. I'll call you later at home, after the publisher's meeting."

* * *

Quietly he dropped the handset into its cradle. He sat a moment with his hand on the instrument as if prolonging the connection to his caller. When he looked up, Jack appeared to be deep in thought as he looked over the paper he held.

"Sorry about the interruption, Jack."

"No problem. I know what it's like to try and get together with a girlfriend. Schedules are deadly these days. And the demands for our time can be endless."

Mac looked at him, radar on alert. "Oh, Emily isn't a girlfriend. She's a colleague working on a project with me." Mac stood up and offered Jack his handshake. "Thanks for the info on advertising strategies. And, I commend you and Amanda for how well the personals are going. I know it can be a tough department and you're doing a great job."

"We do our best, boss." Jack returned the handshake firmly. His voice was much more mellow than at the beginning of the meeting. "Anything else or can I get back to work?"

"No, that's great, Jack. Thanks for your time and input."

* * *

Jack quickly left the room, pulling Mac's door shut behind him. Mac tapped his index finger against his lip as he watched the man leave. Jack had buttons that could be pushed. And women succeeding was clearly a hot issue for him.

But is he a serial rapist about to raise the stakes in a depraved game?

Mac reviewed their conversation. Jack had been the most relaxed when he thought he was leading Mac where he wanted him to go. The editor paused a moment as he remembered the phone call interrupting them, and the questions Jack had asked about Emily. At that moment, Mac had sensed a hunter's adrenaline rush coming from the man.

He hoped he'd seriously defused Jack's strange and sudden interest in Emily. Mac tapped his chin with one finger. One thing he did know. Emily was not going to Breadstix with Jack, if that's who her date was, without Mac there.

"Hell," he muttered, "I don't care if the whole room is full of cops. I'll be there when she faces down the bastard."

* * *

Outside Mac's office, Jack leaned against the door panel, grinning. If only that moron knew how he'd used his precious newspaper to find his prey.

Jack was intrigued by Mac's conversation with the colleague, Emily. He licked his lips. Mac was probably sleeping with her. And she was some built blonde who decorated Landon's designer-suited arm at management dinners. *Huh, worthless slut more than likely.*

Perhaps when he was done with his newest quarry, he'd find out more about Emily. Teach that arrogant Mac a lesson about who was in charge. It would be his reward for exerting such self-control the night before as he'd baited his trap and noticed Mac wandering around the newspaper office.

Jack shoved off the door and trotted back to his desk. He looked around. Amanda was on the phone with a client and no one else was paying him attention. Time to check his phone messages. Jack punched in the numbers to his new phone number.

He knew that if officials learned his prey had been dating through the personals, they'd check her phone records. It was important no one could link him to the redhead, so he was covering his tracks. He'd rented a hotel room in a seedy part of town that didn't ask for references. Wearing a disguise, he'd paid cash for the pest-ridden dump and signed the lease for a month. But he'd never use the room. He just needed its phone line so Emma would have a number to call. And a voice mail system to receive her messages.

The computer voice advised him that he had one new message. He stabbed in the numbers of his code.

As her soft words poured into his ear, he grunted with pleasure. Soon that voice would be saying whatever words he demanded. A cold smile curled his lips. That sultry voice would be begging for Emma's life.

So excited he dared not move, he listened to her message three times before he hung up. He memorized every word and the phone number linking her to him.

Quickly Jack dialed the number she'd left. A machine answered. For some reason, he didn't mind that she was unavailable to him at the moment. She must be at work. She'd get his message when she arrived home, and would be alone to anticipate their evening together. He quivered at the prospect.

"Hello, Emma. Andrew here. I was delighted to get your message on my machine. Isn't this just the way things go these days? Our machines making our plans?" He laughed lightly. "I'd love to meet you for dinner at Breadstix tomorrow night. I've dined there a couple of times and enjoyed it, but I think tomorrow evening, I'll find it even more charming. I'll look forward to meeting you at seven-thirty. Until then." He hung up and sagged in the chair, blood pumping in his veins.

Tomorrow night. He would have her tomorrow night.

A meal together in public would be followed by his physical mastery of her. Unlike the others, he didn't need or want her trust. That wasn't part of this new game. But he did need to control her body and her mind. Tomorrow night, he would fulfill that need.

The fact that the night signaled the beginning of a weekend worked perfectly for him No one would miss him at work. He wouldn't have to leave the apartment for two days.

She would be so much fun for him. He let his mind conjure the picture of her walking away from him in the lobby of the newspaper. Emma's body might as well have been naked he could see her so clearly as she glided across the marble floor on muscular, fit legs. If she chose to fight him, she would be a worthy adversary. But he didn't doubt his ability to bring her down.

She would be a fit prize for him.

Glancing around, he noticed Amanda waving to him. Line two was ringing. With a nod to her, he picked it up. Another ad begging for love awaited him.

CHAPTER 13

Emily dropped the phone into the handset in shock. Right this minute Mac was talking to a possible suspect in the Yorkton rapes. She and Mac had even discussed the fact that Jack was a candidate.

How could he think of talking to Jack?

If he tipped their hand or even gave a hint, and Jack was the man they were searching for, the suspect would go so far underground, they'd never find him. And he'd take his rage with him. Some other woman might suffer from his increasing lack of control, heightened by his anger at being threatened.

Emily began to shake. She paused and took a deep, calming breath. Mac knew what he was doing. She reminded herself of what she'd learned about him from Ryan and others. How he'd gone undercover for his stories in the past, how he'd infiltrated a huge drug cartel to get a story from the inside. Drug lords were highly dangerous people with vital secrets they'd kill to keep. Mac had earned their trust *and* helped shut down one of the biggest importers in the city.

She'd also heard how Mac had been a confidante of beat cops, never once betraying a secret or a source. Yes, Mac knew what he was doing.

Besides, she reminded herself, he was Jack's boss and it would seem strange if he avoided an employee. It was probably just a routine meeting. Pushing down her fear, she headed for Barbara's office.

"Emily, hold up a second," Angela called out, hurrying along the corridor to catch up to her.

"What's up?"

"We just got a hit on Emma's answering machine."

"Is it him?"

"Sure is. I've paged Ryan and was on my way to get Barbara."

Barbara's door stood partway open and Emily tapped on it as she stuck her head inside. "Barbara, it's him."

"You sure?" she asked.

"Andrew calling for Emma," responded Angela. "It's got to be him."

After flipping shut the file folder she was reading, the psychologist jumped up and joined the other women as they entered the boardroom. Ryan was already seated at the conference table.

He looked up as they walked in. "So, have we really hooked him?"

"Oh, I'd say he's definitely interested," commented Angela as she closed the door and slid into a chair. She hit the play button on the portable tape recorder she was carrying. A cool, well-educated voice filled the room. They listened intently. When he stopped speaking, everyone turned to Barbara.

"That's him," she stated. "Listen to his word choices. He hasn't *eaten* at Breadstix, he's dined there. He isn't looking forward to the evening, he's expecting it to be charming. He's even philosophical about the answering machines. Although I wouldn't count on that being a constant for any length of time. If Emma's the woman he's stalking now, he'll quickly become irritated if he continues to get the machine rather than Emma, herself." She looked around the room. "Any comments?"

"Just one," said Emily. "We've got him in our sites. Let's make sure we take him down before anything spooks him."

"Did anyone trace this call?" Ryan asked.

"It's a downtown hotel. Yesterday, the room was rented out for a month. Guy paid in cash and the clerk can't even tell us how tall he was. Just that he paid in cash." Angela looked around. "I think the room's just a drop for the phone line."

"Agreed," said Emily. "But let's put a couple of uniforms in the area, just in case. Now, how do we handle tomorrow night?"

"Just the way we've planned all along," Ryan said. "You have dinner with the cretin while Angela and I keep an eye on things. If all goes well after a couple of dates, we'll set you up at the safe house, stake it out and wait for him to arrive."

"I want to make certain we collect evidence at the safe house that'll put this animal behind bars for the rest of his life. I'll bet he didn't just start preying on women when he moved here. He's gotten away with this crap for years. I'm sure we'll find unsolved rape cases in every city where he's lived."

"So what are you saying?"

"We've got to let him get his hands on me."

Her comment was instantly greeted by a chorus of voices.

"No way," yelled Ryan.

"You remember we think he's planning to kill this time?" Barbara's voice was raised in fear.

"Emily, be smart. He'll try to rape you," Angela pleaded.

Emily banged the table with her hand in an attempt to regain quiet. "I don't mean let him attack or rape me. But if we arrest him in the yard of the safe house, what is he? A peeping tom? A trespasser? No way. This guy is dangerous and vicious. I want him stopped in his tracks now. For that, we need rock solid evidence. Look, I'm not being stupid about this. I don't intend to take even a little chance. I'm certainly not going to be alone with him.

"We'll all be wired. I want Ryan in the closet and I want Barbara behind a two way mirror that'll look like an ordinary dresser mirror. She can monitor his behavior and stay in contact using the radio transmitters in our ears. Angela, your assignment will be tough because you won't be able to see what's going on very well. I want you under the bed so you take him from below while Ryan nails him from across the room. We'll have officers outside in the yard."

"It's still awfully dangerous," counseled the psychologist. "He'll be cautious about his movements." She paused, thinking for a moment. "*And* he'll be incredibly treacherous when he figures out what's happening to him. Be prepared for him to be armed and extremely dangerous."

"That's why we've got to get him in the bedroom with the tools of his trade—a knife, rope, tape, whatever. It's our only chance to build a real case against him."

"Well, you're right that just finding him in the yard won't result in much of a case against him, especially with the lack of physical evidence he's left at other scenes." Angela looked at Emily. "You can count on me to do my part."

"I won't hesitate to take him down," stated Ryan with a frown. "This pond scum is done in this town."

"Okay, so we're agreed," said Emily.

"Agreed," they chorused.

Emily looked around the room at the people who would protect her life. Every one of them knew that once the suspect realized he was about to be arrested, he'd go for Emily. His final action would probably be his attempt to kill her.

She took a deep breath. "Now, I've just got to pretend to buy his charm and his story tomorrow night at dinner. Once we've been on a couple of dates, I'll become less careful about keeping my address secret. Slowly, I'll release details so he can find the safe house."

They nodded in tense agreement, then reviewed their arrangements for Friday night one more time. Everything had to be perfect. Emily's life depended on it.

* * *

Emily was exhausted when she arrived home. All she could think about was warm, bubbly water soaking around her aching shoulders. She stretched one arm over her head and then the other, trying to lessen some of the tension, but she knew she wouldn't really relax again until she had Andrew, or whatever his real name was, in custody. She rotated her head gently on her neck, closing her eyes and enjoying the sensation. She wandered down the hall into the bathroom.

Emily opened the faucets to the perfect temperature and started filling the tub. Into it, she poured a generous handful of aroma-therapy oil designed to help her unwind. She watched the bubbles boil up in an ecstasy of fragrance. Suddenly she remembered a partial bottle of wine sitting in the fridge. The thought of sipping its icy sweetness as she soaked in the scented froth seemed irresistible. Soon, a crystal glass stood waiting on the tiny table at the edge of the tub, its golden liquid shimmering in the reflection of clustered lit candles.

Ambling back to the living room, Emily looked over her selection of music. Chopin suited her mood perfectly and she loaded a disc into the player. The sounds flowed down the hall to the bathroom, which now resembled a spa.

Satisfied, Emily began to disrobe. As each layer disappeared, a little of the day's stress eased.

Ready to slip into the waiting bath water, she sighed in contentment and stretched. It had been a hard day, but soon her assignment would be complete and the city would be safer. As she collected her favorite terry robe, her eye caught the portable phone. The machine could answer. Then Barbara's comments flooded into her mind that he'd become angered by a machine.

"He doesn't have this number," Emily reminded herself aloud. "But Mac does, and maybe he'll call if the meeting ends early." The thought of talking to Mac made her feel better. She picked up the cordless phone and took it into the bathroom.

Emily climbed into the inviting froth of warm, perfumed water. As it closed over her, Emily felt the last of the day's worries slipping away. She picked up the glass and sipped. She was so close to the end. By this time next week, the guy would be in custody. She let it go.

Emily's mind drifted easily to Mac. Once this was over, they'd be free to explore their feelings for one another. It just seemed natural to think of the future and Mac together. She felt a tiny smile curl her lips as she remembered the passion that had risen so quickly between them the night before. She knew exactly what would have happened if the press room hadn't called.

Emily sipped the wine and let her head rest gently against the ceramic tile. She closed her eyes and floated back to Mac's study. She had been in his arms, his warm hands caressing her back. Her hands unbuttoned his shirt, found his skin…

The phone rang. With a frown, she reached for it. "Hello?"

"Hi, it's me. Do you have a few minutes?" Mac's voice was intimate and warm.

"I sure do," Emily answered sinking back into the bubbly water. "I thought you had a meeting tonight."

"We're taking a break for dinner, but I wasn't hungry for food. My mind kept going back to last evening."

"It was a nice dinner, wasn't it?" Emily teased, knowing exactly what he meant.

"Yes, it was. I'm just sorry we had to miss dessert."

Emily felt the thrill of desire vibrate through her. She swallowed another sip of wine before she answered. "And what would you have ordered, Mac? Something with whipped cream perhaps? Or are you a fan of chocolate sauce?"

She heard the hissed intake of his breath and smiled at her power over him

After a moment's silence, his voice flowed down the phone line like liquid silk. "There's nothing wrong with chocolate sauce and whipped cream together. In fact, I can imagine where each belongs on that gorgeous body of yours." He paused and she heard him swallow. "I do believe we would have ended up making sundaes most of the night if we hadn't been interrupted."

"Funny you should say that, Mac. I was just lying here thinking about last night."

His voice was hoarse. "Are you in bed?"

"No, not exactly," she whispered, splashing the water so he could hear. "I'm in a big tub full of warm, scented bubbles. Music's playing and I'm sipping wine as I think about what might have been last night."

"Tub?" It was all he could seem to get out.

"Um-hum. I've got candles burning and the mood is just right." She sat up and purposely sloshed the water so he could hear. "Now, I'm sitting up, Mac. I'm only waist-deep in water." She heard a gargling sound coming from the phone. "The bubbles are covering me. But I'm getting cold." She let him think of the imagery. "Since I'm all by myself, I think I'd better slide back into this warm, soapy water. Want to come over and wash my back?" She put on her best southern drawl. "And my front, of course?"

His voice sounded strangled. "I want to be there in that tub with you covered in bubbles and champagne, Emily. I want to run my warm, slippery hands over every inch of you." She gasped gently as he continued. "I want you to sit between my legs while I shampoo your hair, while I soap those perfect breasts and run my hands the length of your beautiful legs. Then I want us to slip under the water together and rinse off. I want you to kneel in front of me and cover me in bubbles from head to toe. I want your hands on every part of me. Do you understand that I mean *all* of me? I want you to touch me everywhere while I explore you."

Emily moaned softly as he continued to whisper what he'd like to do with her and to her. The wine glass slipped from her limp fingers and she gasped as icy wine splashed over her breasts.

"What happened?" Mac asked.

"My wine spilled."

"Where?"

"Down my front."

"If I were there I'd lap it off your skin. Then I'd gather you into a huge towel and carry you to the bedroom where I'd gently dry your body and tuck you into bed."

"But you must join me," Emily invited.

"Of course, my darling. I'm wanting you so badly that nothing will do but to slide under those covers with you. Then I can use my hands, my mouth and my body to show you how much you mean to me." He groaned softly. "I can feel the velvet of your skin and the peaks of your nipples already. I can feel your slick wetness when I finally embrace you the way I long to—under me, around me. A part of me."

Her sigh caressed his ear. "Come over tonight, Mac. I want you so much I don't want to wait any longer."

"If I could, I would. But this meeting is going on 'til sometime after midnight."

"Thanks to you, I'll still be wide awake after midnight," she said with a giggle. "Well, if it can't be tonight, meet me here tomorrow evening after my date. I can't wait any longer for us to be together."

"Neither can I."

"I'll see you tomorrow around ten. And Mac," she whispered seductively into the phone. "Just so you have something to think about beside dry publishing statistics, I think I'll get out of the tub." She stood up so he could hear the water dripping into the tub. "I'm going to towel off and rub on some lotion before I climb between the sheets wearing nothing but my fantasies about what I want you to do to my body." She heard his rapid breathing before she hung up and began to towel dry.

CHAPTER 14

Emily buttoned her trench coat over the designer business suit she was wearing to dinner. It fit like a glove. What a shame to return it to the police department's storeroom after her date. Emily knew she'd never afford a suit like this on her salary.

Tonight, she had to remember she was a highly successful architect. They'd set up the cover with a downtown firm where Ryan's sister was a partner. If anyone called looking for Emma Poston, they'd be sent to her voice mail. If anyone showed up, Emma was on a conference call to Europe and wouldn't be available for several hours.

With a final glance in the mirror, Emily grabbed her handbag and headed for the door. Even though the police car, disguised as a cab, would take her to and from the restaurant, neither Emily nor anyone on the team felt their suspect would track her down at this first date. They agreed the real danger would arise when Andrew wanted to come to her home, or perhaps when he invited her away for a weekend. Tonight's date was to get the man's mettle.

Emily climbed into the back seat of the cab in her driveway. "Well, we're off to Breadstix, Joe."

The sergeant behind the wheel grinned and doffed his hat. He seemed to be enjoying his role. The two chatted amicably as they traveled across town to the designated restaurant.

When she walked into the foyer, Emily was relaxed and totally into her persona. She stopped at the entrance to the main salon and looked around. Ryan and Angela were in position, but neither one of them acknowledged her appearance.

Then she started in surprise. Seated in an alcove with a perfect view of the restaurant were Barbara…and Mac.

What's going on?

But she couldn't attempt to speak to them…not enough time before Andrew arrived. Emily swung her eyes to the table she'd reserved and was once again startled. There was already a man seated at the table. She narrowed her eyes.

So, he wants to play control games, does he?

His back faced her, so Emily knew he hadn't spotted her. She stepped back into the main foyer and signaled to the maitre d'.

"Hi, I'm Emma Poston and I have a reservation for 7:30."

"Yes, Ms. Poston. Your guest has already arrived. Even though it's a bit early, we have seated him already."

"I see that. And his early arrival is"—she paused—"unexpected. I'll be in the bar for the next half hour."

Even as she made her plans, Emily knew it was a juvenile response to the two surprises. But she needed time to regain her equilibrium. This guy needed to understand she wasn't meekly playing his game.

Emily slipped into a quiet corner of the bar and ordered a ginger ale. She sipped it, and slowly her temper subsided. Mac was only looking out for her safety; he must have argued convincingly for Barbara to play along with him. And if Andrew wanted to play a control game, he could wait until 7:29, believing he had her off guard.

Emily finished the last of her ginger ale and walked into the restaurant foyer. At precisely 7:30, the maitre d' showed her to the table.

She smiled into the slightly irritated face at the table and held out her hand. "Hi, I'm Emma Poston."

"Andrew Morrison," he responded automatically rising to his feet. "How do you do?"

"Great. How nice you're as punctual as I am," Emily praised. "It's 7:30 right on the button. I hate it when people can't tell time, don't you?" Her smile thawed her words

*   *   *

Jack almost believed she was taunting him, but how could that be? She couldn't possibly know he'd just spent the most boring half hour of his life sampling an insipid chablis and planning to belittle her tardiness. In fact, he was forced to acknowledge that she'd arrived at the table exactly when she was supposed to be there.

And to cap off his misery, he'd spotted his boss, Mac Landon, having dinner with some strait-laced looking woman. Their table was covered in paperwork and their heads had been together the whole time. At least he'd been spared any further boredom since Mac had not noticed him.

Jack smiled at his date. "Punctuality is a personal goal. I think I got if from spending so much time at the beach. The tide waits for no one."

"Oh, you've lived near water?"

"My parents had a place on Cape Cod when I was growing up."

"How delightful!" Emily gushed. "I adore the ocean."

"As do I," Jack exclaimed happily. He looked at her and tilted his head. "Do I know you from somewhere? I swear we've met before."

Emily looked at him. "You do seem familiar, but I meet so many people."

"Wait." He pretended to think for a moment, then snapped his fingers. "We met at the newspaper office!"

Emily's gaze was searching. Then suddenly she brightened. "That's right. On the elevator. It was the day we'd each placed our personal ads." She laughed and he felt the laughter's light splinter over him like glass. This was almost too easy. She looked at him and said, "We really got our money's worth. Look how quickly we found each other."

"Really. I can't believe it, can you?"

"No, it seems like such a coincidence." She smiled at him. "But a very nice one. So, Andrew, what do you do for a living?"

"I'm a contractor."

"How interesting. Have I seen any of your buildings?" As their conversation flowed, each seemed oblivious to all around them except one another.

* * *

Mac focused on the table across the room from him. He watched every detail of how Jack moved, how he leaned into Emily as he spoke and how she responded. She was playing her part well, not even her body language betraying her true feelings.

He felt every reporter's instinct sending him violent warning alarms. Jack was dangerous. It was obvious he'd been using the newspaper to stalk his victims and he was definitely planning to make Emily his next trophy.

Mac leaned towards Barbara and murmured, "I can't believe I let that son-of-a-bitch handle ads in my personals department. What do you think?"

"I think we have our man. Watch his hand movements…very abrupt. Notice how they cut through the air cleanly? He believes himself in control. And see how he leans in, then pulls back, getting her to follow him physically in the conversation. He is using a technique like a fisherman, waiting until he has her hooked, then reeling her in."

* * *

Jack laughed, laying his hand on Emily's. As he leaned back in his chair, he smiled widely at the young woman. Feeling her heat touch his core, he could barely contain himself and removed his hand.

"Have you ever been sailing in the moonlight?" Jack's voice was meant as a caress.

"No, I'm not really much of a sailboat person," Emily breathed. "I do love to walk on the beach though." She paused and looked up through her eyelashes at him. "I have a collection of shells from every beach I've ever walked on." She laughed gently. "You must think me silly."

"Actually," he leaned forward, placing his hand over hers again. "I don't. I have one special shell from each of my favorite beaches. They take me right back to the moment I found it, when I held it in my hand. I've never told anyone that," he confided, looking deeply into her eyes. "I always thought people would laugh at me."

The waiter arrived with their meals.

* * *

Emily shimmered with relief. She could not stomach his hand on hers. His skin was hot and dry, and she felt trapped when he touched her. Picking up her fork and spoon, she forced a smile and began to twist the pasta expertly.

He returned her smile as he cut into his blue-rare steak and lifted a piece of meat to his mouth. Emily barely controlled a shiver as he forked the bloody morsel into his mouth, then dabbed his lips with his napkin.

A sudden crash sounded at the kitchen door as two waiters collided, each carrying a full tray of dishes. People twisted in their seats to see what had happened, Emily among them. As she turned back to her dinner date, she noticed he had bent down to the floor and was just settling back into his seat.

He held up his napkin. "The sound startled me and I dropped this under the table."

She repressed a shudder at the blood staining the white linen. "Well, it sure made me jump," she agreed, turning back to her meal.

As the evening continued, Emily sensed the man across the table withdraw. He was still charming and pleasant, but slightly more distant than at the beginning of the evening when he'd flirted so obviously with her. She wondered if he'd decided to take her off his list for some reason. Panic rose.

Is he considering more women than just me for his next prey? Could he have lost interest in me? Or is this a technique to lure me to him?

If it was a ploy to make him more enticing to her, it was working. Emily definitely felt the need to make him want to pursue her. She forced herself to relax.

"So shall we meet again for dinner?" she asked, draining the last of her coffee.

"I think that might be nice." He looked straight at her. "But I'm out of town for a few days next week, so perhaps we shouldn't schedule anything right now."

"Of course. But that makes it all the more interesting, don't you think? Now we get to think about each other for a few days and see if the attraction is really there." Emily's challenge seemed to strike a nerve.

"Oh, I do believe the attraction is there." He leaned forward and touched her hand once more. "I can certainly feel it."

Emily kept the smile tucked inside. So this was a ploy and she'd passed.

She let the smile spread across her lips and turned her hand under his so their palms met. "I do, too, Andrew. I have to admit, I don't think I've ever met anyone quite like you."

She saw his bloodlust flare. His eyes turned silvery and unfocused, as if thrilling to an imagined tableau. It was a frightening thing to behold. A moment later, he'd recovered, returning her smile. His veneer of civilization had slid back into place.

"I haven't felt anything quite like this in a very long time," he whispered, his forefinger stroking her palm intimately. "I'll very much look forward to getting together again as soon as possible after I return."

She smiled and didn't say anything, but bent to retrieve her purse from under the table. As she stood, he bounded to his feet and pulled back her chair for her. Walking across the restaurant, she noticed Mac and Barbara still engrossed in whatever papers covered their table, but Ryan and Angela were already putting on their coats in the foyer.

His hand slid to the small of her back as he guided her toward the coat rack. Emily turned and smiled up at him, leaned slightly closer to him as they walked among the tables. In the foyer, he helped her on with her coat before slipping into his. Ryan and Angela were lingering at the door and he turned to them, glaring. He obviously wanted to be alone with her.

The two officers took the hint and left.

Jack stood in front of Emily and slid his hand up the lapels of her trench coat, taking hold of the collar just below her throat. "I'm so glad we found each other, Emma," he said in a low voice. "I get the feeling you're the one I've been waiting for."

"It is like fate, isn't it? I know you're the man I've been searching for." *It wasn't a lie.*

He tilted his body toward hers and blocked her view of the people around her. His hands never left her coat as he tugged her closer to him. He pressed his body against the length of hers and let her feel his physical excitement. Then, just as he seemed to sense her rising concern, he stepped back and brushed a finger across her lips.

"I know it's too soon to ask to see you home, but let me get you a cab," he offered.

"Thank you, Andrew. That would be great," she managed to get out around her rising gorge.

They stepped onto the sidewalk and he signaled to the police cab waiting for her. It pulled up and they walked to it, her arm tucked into his. Holding the door for her, he couldn't seem to control his lust and his hand brushed her breast.

Emily started and looked at him questioningly.

"My apologies. May I call you when I get back from out of town?"

"Of course. I'll look forward to our next meeting."

He closed the car door and the cab pulled away from the curb.

* * *

Jack stepped into the shadow of the building. Reaching into his pocket, he pulled out a tiny electronic device. The screen glowed green with a brighter green dot moving across its surface.

He bared his teeth. She'd see him much sooner than she expected and in ways she certainly never anticipated.

He gestured to another cab and climbed in, watching as the green dot on his tracking device lead him straight to his quarry's lair. Without haste, he followed her electronic trail.

CHAPTER 15

Emily heaved a sigh of relief as the police officer drove her home. Leaning her head back against the seat, she said, "It worked, Joe. It worked."

"That's great, Emily. So you think he'll call again?"

"For absolutely, positively sure, this guy will call. It's just a matter of time now before we have him exactly where we want him—in jail!"

When Joe pulled up in front of her house, Emily got out with a quick good-night to her fellow officer and headed into the house. She flicked off the outside lights and locked the door behind her. She was exhausted. It had been a stressful, but successful night. All she could think about was a good night's sleep.

Tomorrow she'd talk to Mac and Barbara, and find out just what they'd thought they were doing showing up at Breadstix and throwing her off. The sting was set up well; it didn't need their participation.

Mac! She'd forgotten he was planning to come over.

Kicking off her shoes in the front foyer, Emily wandered into the kitchen. She dialed Mac's home phone and poured herself a large glass of orange juice, then slung the suit jacket over the back of a chair. In a minute, the skirt was tossed on top of the jacket.

No answer. He was probably taking Barbara home. She left him a message that she was exhausted and would call him in the morning.

As Emily made her way down the hall to the bedroom, she unclasped her bra, letting the feeling of freedom roll over her as she shed the constricting undergarment. Bra dangling from one finger and glass of orange juice in the other hand, Emily turned off the hall light and made her way to her room in the glow of the streetlights. She set the half-empty glass on her night stand and sank down on the bed to remove pantyhose and panties.

Naked, she pattered into her bathroom and washed her face clean of Emma's makeup. She slid a cotton knee-length nightie over her head and headed back to her bedroom, intent on a good night's sleep. She turned back the covers, finished the juice, and climbed into bed. Moments after pulling up the covers around her shoulders, she was asleep.

*　　*　　*

Smiling, he stared at her through the window. It had been more than he'd hoped for when she'd walked into the bedroom topless. Then she'd sat right in front him and disrobed, almost like she was doing it just for him. He decided he'd have her repeat the performance once she was safely in his lair.

She had a spectacular body—as good as he'd imagined. Her breasts weren't large, but shapely and upturned with small nipples. He liked that. Looking at her firm, concave abdomen made him so hard he froze. Her butt was almost his undoing as he watched her leave the bedroom.

Emma is perfect.

He started to imagine the ways he'd use her body, barely able to wait until he saw her naked form again.

With disappointment, he watched her return to the bedroom wearing the nightgown. His good mood revived as he thought about having her with him, dressed only in what he'd allowed her to wear. It wouldn't be much. Licking his lips in anticipation, he realized only a short time existed before she would be his.

He stood patiently in the shadows as she fell asleep. He waited a bit longer. Then he slipped on latex gloves, coveralls and the bathing cap he always used, grabbed the bag beside him and crept to the kitchen door. It was locked, but that stopped him only temporarily. Few locks stymied him.

He let himself into the kitchen and quietly closed the door. After silently rummaging in the bag, he pulled out the cloth and rope. For a moment, he held the knife in his hand, but returned it to the bag with a grimace. He wouldn't need it here.

Straightening, he spotted the suit on the back of the chair. He couldn't resist picking it up and sniffing. It still bore the fragrance of her body and he ached again at his immediate reaction to her. He rubbed the softness of the suit against himself, then dropped it on the chair. He was wasting time when he could have the real thing. Stealing down the hall, he glanced in each room, checking for other occupants. Not that they'd stop him, but he preferred to leave no traces of Emma's abduction.

At the door to her bedroom, he paused. She was no more than ten feet away from him, sound asleep with the covers tucked around her shoulders against the chill of the evening. Her mouth was slightly open and he could see her tongue behind her bottom teeth in the dim glow from the street light. He crept over to the bed and dropped the cloth onto her face. She didn't waken.

Jack wanted to see her eyes recognize him. He pressed down on the cloth.

Her eyes flew open. They filled with fear as she recognized him.

Then her stare changed and her hands came up to his. For a moment, she pushed against him before she seemed to realize that wasn't working. She dropped her hands to her chest and he thought she'd given up.

Suddenly, the heel of her hand lashed out to his solar plexus. He gasped at the quick, crushing thump and reached for the damaged area. She tore the cloth from her mouth and inhaled a lungful of fresh air.

Jack smiled. This was more than he'd hoped for. Even from her.

He snatched the cloth and forced it back over her mouth. This time, he stood so she couldn't reach him with fists or knees.

She held her breath, waiting for her moment.

Jack chuckled. She was good, but he was better. Holding the cloth firmly in place with one hand, he grabbed her hair. She knew what was coming. He could see it in her eyes as she braced herself for the pain. He twisted her hair first one way and then the other, finally jerking her head over the edge of the bed.

She still refused to inhale.

He tipped back Emily's head and slid his knee over the hair, holding her head over the bed's edge, cloth still clapped in place. Looking down, he saw her frightened eyes and grinned. He pinched her nostrils shut, shrugging at her. It was only a matter of time until she'd have to inhale. Then, the anesthetic would do its work and she'd lose consciousness within seconds.

She closed her eyes and let her mouth fall open. Because he was pushing so firmly against the cloth, his index finger and thumb automatically slid into her mouth.

Emily bit down hard.

"Damn you!" He tore his hand from her punishing teeth and slapped her hard across the cheekbone. The cloth fell from her face at his violent movement. Tears started from her eyes at the sudden pain.

"That's just the beginning for you," he snarled, grabbing her arms and twisting them cruelly behind her back as he rolled her face down into the bedding. Again, he forced the cloth over her mouth and nose. Emily struggled futilely, but was soon forced to breathe.

Jack felt her body go limp under his hands. He held the cloth in place for several more breaths to be sure she was totally under. Then he rolled her over and smoothed her hair gently away from her face. He could already see the bruise forming on her cheekbone where he'd struck her.

Why did Emma force me to mar her so soon?

Her nightgown had ridden up in the struggle and Jack began to pull it back down. His hands brushed against the curls between her legs. It took all his will power to not play with her body. Jack reminded himself that he was the ultimate hunter. He'd take his prize to his lair where nothing would interrupt him.

Working quickly, Jack bound her hands and feet with the rope. Then he laid her gently on the floor. He made the bed so it looked like she'd never been in it. Crouching, he picked up Emily and slung her over his shoulder, fireman style. Even as dead weight, she was easy for him to carry.

Back in the kitchen, Jack laid her on the floor again and took care of his equipment. He returned the cloth to its plastic bag. No point in two of them passing out, he thought with a grin as he sealed the bag and dropped it into the carryall. He glanced around, searching for her purse, and found it lying on a chair. He groped in the side pocket and, after a moment, pulled out a tiny transmitter.

He barely felt the sharp stab through his glove from a pin in her purse.

After dropping the bug into his bag, he locked the kitchen door from the inside and pulled Emily's keys off the hook beside the door leading to the garage.

In his excitement, he didn't see the specks of blood he left on the wall below the key rack.

Jack carried Emily to the garage, unlocked her car and propped her up in the front passenger seat. He hooked the seatbelt firmly around her.

Back in the kitchen, he retrieved his bag and looked around quickly. Nothing had been left behind.

Jack locked the door to the garage from the garage side. *Might as well make it look like Emma was doing all this*. He climbed into the car, started it and hit the garage door opener. After backing out the car, he triggered the device to return the door to its place. There would be no suspicion of anything wrong at Emma Poston's. No neighbors would call the police over the weekend.

Jack backed out of the driveway and headed down the street. It had been almost too easy. He looked in the rear view mirror. No one was following.

He smiled and clicked on the radio to his favorite station. The only challenge now was to get Emma into his apartment unseen. Even that presented very little problem because of the underground parking. And the fact that he'd bribe the doorman to take a break after telling his story of bringing home a very reclusive, very married lady to his apartment. If any night owls were arriving home late, he merely had to rouse Emma to semi-consciousness and walk her to his apartment. Anyone who saw them would assume the lady was slightly inebriated. After that....

The sound-proofed room awaited her.

*　　*　　*

As Mac pulled up to Emily's, he saw the garage door opening. Instinctively, he turned off his headlights. He watched as her car backed out, paused while the door slid back into place, then backed toward the road. Maybe Emily was headed to the station for some reason, even though they'd planned to meet. But his intuition told him that was not the case. Mac hunched behind the wheel.

Just for a moment, the driver was backlit by the streetlight. It was not a woman driving the car. Mac stared intently into the passenger compartment. He saw a person, there, slumped at an unnatural angle. Without a moment's hesitation, Mac grabbed his cell phone and punched in the number for Emily's precinct.

As the car began to leave, he slipped his Jaguar into gear and slid into the street behind them. Staying far enough back to avoid suspicion, Mac waited impatiently for the duty officer to answer.

"Officer Simms, here," said the crisp voice.

"Oh, Dave, it's Mac Landon."

"Mac." The voice warmed considerably. "What can I do for you?"

"Is Emily scheduled to come in tonight?"

There was a rustle of paper. "Nope, she's not back on duty until Monday, according to the roster."

"We may have a bit of a problem then." Mac described what he'd just witnessed. "Not that she can't lend someone her car, but there was a second person in the passenger seat and I'm not sure that everything is ok. Can you send someone around to her house to check it out?"

"You got it." Simms' voice became muffled as he turned his mouth away from the phone and began barking orders.

"And Dave," said Mac when the cop came back on the line, "you may want to treat it like a crime scene. If I'm right, she's been abducted."

"What? Do you know who has her?"

"I'm not certain, but I'm on their track. It may be the suspect her task force has been investigating."

"The rapist?"

"I'm afraid so. I don't want to spook this guy with a load of police cars bearing down on him. I'm headed east –" With a click, Mac's phone went dead. He banged it helplessly against the dashboard. "Hello?" Still nothing.

The battery was dead. And he didn't have the luxury of time to stop at a payphone. At all costs, he couldn't lose them.

Mac had no idea where Jack lived, no idea where he was taking Emily. He squinted ahead. They still moved toward downtown. He'd have to take the chance of getting a bit closer to them. He pressed down on the accelerator and the powerful car answered, easily closing the gap between the vehicles. Mac slid into the lane, two cars back from Jack.

Fifteen minutes later, Jack swung into the underground parking garage of an apartment building not too far from the newspaper office. Mac drove by and pulled up to the curb in case it was a ruse to throw him off the path. He waited ten minutes before he was satisfied Jack wasn't leaving. Then he swung the car back into traffic and drove the two blocks to the newspaper's parking lot. His car wouldn't be spotted there.

Leaping out of his car, Mac considered running into the office building and calling the police. But he'd already left Jack alone with Emily for nearly fifteen minutes and he couldn't take the chance Jack wouldn't rape and murder her in the garage.

Even though Barbara was convinced he'd want to toy with his prey like a cat with a mouse, Mac wasn't certain Jack could contain himself. And that could cost Emily her life.

Please God, let there be a phone in the apartment building lobby.

CHAPTER 16

Emily gradually became conscious of movement around her. She wasn't in her bed anymore. Where was she? And why was she moving?

She kept her eyes closed from an instinctive sense of self-preservation, aware of discomfort and the lack of sensation in her hands and legs. Her eyes slid open a slit. She was looking out the front windshield of a car, on a sharp angle.

Carefully keeping her left eye closed so the driver wouldn't realize she was awake, Emily opened her right eye. They were headed downtown, but she couldn't identify their exact location. The right side of her head was pressed against the passenger window; she didn't dare straighten to get a better view.

Growing more alert, Emily searched her memory to discover what had happened. She remembered coming home, drinking a glass of juice and getting ready for bed. She recalled crawling between the sheets and falling asleep almost instantly, too tired to review the night's stake out.

She swallowed deeply as she relived the sudden, hot fear striking her as she awakened with a drug-soaked cloth over her face. She struggled with the image of the person holding the cloth, then bit the inside of her mouth to keep from crying out in terror when she remembered.

Andrew.

The man she'd had dinner with; the one her task force believed was preparing to murder his next victim.

How did he find me?

She knew she hadn't been followed from the restaurant. Emily's mind ticked sluggishly as she searched for the answer. It seemed just beyond her ability to catch it. *Something about dinner.* She hadn't left the table. She'd been careful to prevent him seeing her identification with her address on it. The answer was there. Somewhere.

She heard a crash in her memory. *What was it about a crashing sound at Breadstix?* Emily sighed and felt the driver look at her.

His hand reached over and stroked her breast so pitifully protected by the thin cotton of her nightgown. It was all she could do not to shudder in revulsion at his touch. But if he knew she was awake, there was no telling what he'd do. She had to stall for time to figure out a way to escape him.

"Nice," she heard him murmur, lust thick in his voice. "Very nice and all mine."

She swallowed nervously, struggling to stay focused as the drugs she'd inhaled swirled through her brain. Several minutes passed. The car suddenly swung left, descending into an underground parking garage. Wherever he was taking her, they were almost there. Her heart pounded in dread at what must be coming next.

For some reason, it became essential to figure out how he'd found her. Her mind wove back over the evening. *Why was a crash so important?* And then it struck her. When everyone else had turned to the sound of the waiters' over-laden trays colliding, Andrew hadn't. He'd been under the table, just straightening up when she turned back to him. He'd held up his napkin and she'd accepted his casual explanation he'd dropped it in surprise at the noise. Now she knew.

He'd dropped a tracking device into her purse. He hadn't had to worry about keeping the cab in sight when she left the restaurant. He'd just followed her signal home. So easy.

She suddenly realized nobody would miss her until the task force debriefing Saturday at noon. Her logical police mind followed the train of thought. He'd have a head start of nearly twelve hours before anyone knew she was missing.

Emily gritted her teeth. That twelve hour period spelled the difference between her life and death. Only her own ability would ensure she survived it. While Emily knew she was well-trained and fit, she also acknowledged she was going to need some luck.

Carefully, she breathed in oxygen as deeply as she could, head tipped as far from her captor as possible. If she could keep one eye open, she might figure out where she was.

The car circled into the depths of the garage. She counted five levels. The building must be large. That could work to her benefit. Surely such a large building would have security personnel or a doorman. If she could just get to one of them!

They turned into a parking space. Emily could make out part of the window sticker on the Mercedes beside them: "…ury Arms Parking Permit."

The sight relieved her. There would be security in a building with permits, and probably surveillance cameras everywhere. If she lived to take advantage of them…

She heard the car turn off and the driver's seatbelt unbuckling. Emily braced herself as the driver's hand slid against her hip and unfastened hers as well. Unless he planned to carry her, a highly suspicious move if they met someone in the elevator or hallway, he'd now have to awaken her. She didn't have to appear alert and make it easy for him. Nothing said the knockout drug didn't have a profound effect on her.

He touched her, but she was expecting that. His hands crept over her nightgown, exploring the curves of her body. She heard him groan once or twice as he rubbed her breasts. Then he flicked a finger across her nipple.

"Come on, Emma, my dear," he crooned obscenely, "time to rise and shine." He laughed at his own crude joke and prodded at each of her breasts in turn, expecting to elicit a response from her if she'd begun to regain consciousness.

Emily steeled herself and remained slumped against the passenger door. Momentarily, she thought he'd given up and then she felt his hand roved over her abdomen and dip lower. She jerked spastically and almost screamed as his fingers dipped under the hem of her nightgown and slid upwards.

"Waking up are you?" He slithered across the seat and ran his hand the length of her thigh.

She shivered and slowly opened her eyes. She stared in amazement. He was wearing a bathing cap, latex gloves and coveralls.

"I'll make sure you're awake enough to walk." His hand crept up her leg. His fingers splayed across her and he looked into her eyes. "Just a preview, my dear Emma, of what's to come."

"Where are we?" Emily deliberately slurred her speech.

"Why, we're almost home. And then we'll have time to play." He leered in her face. "And from what I've seen, we're going to have a very good time together. Oh, yes, a very good time."

"Home?" She looked at him blearily, calculating the distance to his eyes. Just in time, she remembered her hands were bound.

"Don't worry. I've made up a room especially for you. Well, it's what you'll call home for a few days anyway." He bared his teeth in a parody of a smile as his eyes traveled across her body once more. His hands followed suit as he fondled her breasts again. She could see how excited he was.

Emily braced herself as hot fear rippled through her. *Barbara was right. This guy is ready to move from rape to murder.* She shook her head, ostensibly trying to clear the fog from her mind when really, she wanted to distract him from his groping.

"Why do you have me tied up? I can't play if I'm tied up."

"That was just to get you here. You know, in case you didn't want to come with me willingly."

Emily decided to take a chance. "Why wouldn't I be willing to come with you? You did scare me at the house. But"—she licked at her lips—"this is kind of interesting."

She saw the flare of lust. His hands were on her again. Emily pushed her breasts against his hands and moaned, willing herself to pretend to meet his level of excitement.

"Touch me," she whispered.

He groaned as his hands rove over her body, this time at her invitation. Clearly, he hadn't expected this response from her, and appeared to struggle with his control. Now she just had to convince him to untie her. She swung her bound hands towards his chest and fumbled at his shirt buttons. She looked at him helplessly.

"Don't worry. You'll soon be untied, my dear." He pulled a knife from his pocket and she involuntarily shrank back as he pulled open the blade. "What's wrong? Are you afraid I'll cut you?" He ran the tip of the blade along the curve of her jaw, so lightly she could barely feel it. Then he quickly sliced the blade sliced through the ropes.

She rubbed her wrists in an attempt to get back feeling in her fingers. As they began to tingle, Emily massaged her calves and ankles. She would need to move quickly when the opportunity arose.

Emily glanced sideways at her captor. He was staring at her.

"How come you kidnapped me, Andrew?"

"Would you have come willingly with me?"

"Probably not on the first or second date, but I'm hardly celibate." She smiled at him. "Or are you one of those guys who has to be in control all the time?"

"I guess I just might be," he confessed. "Come on. It's time to head upstairs."

"What's upstairs?" She couldn't help the quaver in her voice. She hadn't missed his excitement at her fear.

"My place and I'd love for you to see it." He ran the knife blade over her abdomen before snapping it shut.

"Sure. How about tomorrow after breakfast?" Her smile was weak.

"No." His voice hardened. "I want you to see it right now—tonight. Now sit still." He clambered over her and opened the passenger door. Standing between the two cars, he quickly stripped off his coveralls, bathing cap and gloves. Then, he grabbed her arm and jerked her out of the car.

"Take it easy." She stumbled drunkenly, pulling her arm out of his grasp. "I'm coming."

He slanted a cold glance at her, but didn't attempt to grab her arm again. Emily straightened her spine and tossed her head. She had to throw him off guard and it seemed to nonplus him when she stood up to his caveman tactics.

"Hey, don't you think I'm kind of obvious in nothing but a nightgown?"

"Here." He peeled off his overcoat and threw it over her shoulders.

"Such a gentleman."

He grasped her hand and jerked her forward. "Let's go."

Emily stumbled on purpose as she followed behind him pretending the cement was hard on her bare feet. She strained to see the permit name on any vehicle they passed, but the garage was too dimly lit for her to make out the words. Each time she lagged, he dragged her forward.

Finally they stood before a bank of elevators. He stabbed at the call button and in moments an empty car arrived. Jack stepped in and pulled Emily along with him. She staggered at the entrance and fell sideways, hitting as many of the floor buttons as she could with her upper arm and elbow. She didn't even look to see if she'd been successful, instead leaning down to rub her toes.

"That hurt, Andrew," she pouted. "You made me catch my toe in the gap of the door."

"Sorry," he muttered.

She caught him looking at her through narrowed eyes. *He's wondering if I hit those buttons on purpose.* Emily continued massaging her toes, keeping her head down.

He jabbed at the panel.

As his eyes turned away from her, Emily stole a peek at the elevator panel. He'd just hit the button for the fourteenth floor. But it was the ones she'd managed to reach that caused her heart to pound in glee. Thanks to her "clumsiness" they'd be stopping at all the garage levels. And the lobby.

She straightened and leaned sideways against him. If she could convince him she was playing the game, perhaps he'd let down his guard for just a minute. She could do a lot in that moment.

"So, Andy, have you lived here long?" Emily purred looking up at him.

"A while."

"I can hardly wait to see your place."

"We'll be there in a minute." His tone was surly as the elevator stopped on the second parking level.

"How come we keep stopping?"

"When you fell coming into the elevator, you must've hit a bunch of buttons."

"Oops, sorry." She giggled drunkenly. "Oh, well, you said we'll be there soon."

Just then the elevator glided to a stop again. They were at the lobby. The doors slid open, and Emily stepped out.

She glanced left and right. No one in sight. Not even the doorman. She felt his sudden movement behind her and slumped to the floor, feigning weakness. She became dead weight, forcing him to hoist her up.

With a final desperate look toward the front door, she let him drag her back into the elevator. Just before she lost sight of the foyer, she saw a quick movement at the edge of a window. Then he had her back in the elevator.

Jack shoved her against the back wall. "What the hell were you doing?"

"I thought it was our floor," she whimpered, looking frightened. "I thought you said we'd be there in a minute, so I got out when we stopped. Why are you so mad at me?" She forced her eyes out of focus and wobbled slightly. "I thought it was our floor," she repeated and slid down the wall into a heap on the floor.

She could feel his cold eyes staring at her. Idly, she wondered why the doorman hadn't been at his post.

Quickly the elevator rose to the fourteenth floor and eased to a stop. He twisted a hand into her hair and pulled her to her feet. Tears jetted from her eyes.

"Ouch," she moaned. "You're hurting me."

"Then get to your feet," he snarled in reply. "I want you to walk down this hall. I'm not going to carry you."

With as much dignity as she could muster, Emily tossed back her head and stepped out of the elevator. Slowly, she walked down the hall, weaving only slightly. He had to continue to believe she was suffering from the after effects of the drug he'd used on her.

Emily knew her chances of survival diminished significantly once inside his apartment. She wove away from him again and pitched toward an apartment door. His hand snaked out and closed around her wrist like a manacle.

"Now don't be waking up any of the neighbors, my dear."

"Sorry." She smiled bemusedly at him. "Are we almost there?"

"You seem very anxious to get to my apartment."

She looked at him apologetically. "I really have to use the bathroom."

Looking faintly disgusted, he increased their pace until they were halfway down the corridor. He stopped in front of a door marked 1414 and reached into his pocket. She tensed, preparing to run.

Suddenly, he pulled the trench coat from her shoulders, brandished a knife, and flipped open the blade. After slicing down the front of her nightgown from neck to hem, he grabbed the remnants of the night dress and ripped it off her.

With a frightened glance around her, she clasped her arms across her chest.

"I don't think you'll run off naked into the night. Do you?" He looked at her.

"I certainly wouldn't make a good impression on your neighbors. You know, this is a little nerve-racking, standing like this in the hallway." She let her voice raise and he swung his arm, casually backhanding her.

"Keep your voice down." He continued staring at her and she dropped her eyes.

Jack leisurely searched his key ring for the proper one as she shivered beside him. Finally he found it and unlocked the door, pushing it open. He stood back and gestured for her to precede him. With a final despairing look down the hall, she complied. The sound of the door closing terrified her, but she didn't allow him to see that.

"The powder room is down the hall, second door on the left." He gestured in the proper direction.

"Thanks."

Emily entered the tiny bathroom. After she shut the door, alarm coursed through her as she heard the lock click from the outside. "Hey, what's going on?" She pounded on the door, but there was no answer from the other side.

She swung around, startled, as a door opened behind her. He stood there, smiling, playing with his knife.

"This is the only way out," he said archly.

She kept her eyes down, stepped around him and found herself in a bedroom. But it was like no room she'd been in. Foam soundproofing waffles, like those used in production studios, blanketed the walls and ceiling. Padlocked shutters covered the window. She couldn't find evidence of a closet. A bed stretched before her in the center of the room, with a mirror mounted over it. Across from the bed, video equipment had been set up. Handcuffs lay waiting on a bedside table.

White lace and satin decorated everything. To Emily, the chamber looked like a Victorian nightmare.

A cream-colored chemise and tiny bed jacket sprawled across the bed. Once donned, the ensemble would leave very little to the imagination. A pair of stiletto mules rested on the floor beside the bed.

She shivered.

"I hope you like it." His voice actually sounded sincere.

"It's great, but what's with all the locks and stuff?"

"Well, I want you to stay for a while."

"You intend to lock me in here?" Emily's voice rose despite her best efforts not to panic.

"I'm afraid so, Emma, my dear. I can't let you leave."

"Yes, you can. I told you I'd sleep with you already. You don't have to lock me up." She stared wildly at him. "My mother used to lock me in my room if I was bad." She forced the tears to flow. "I can't be locked in. I can't."

He spoke without emotion. "Yes, you can. And you will be, so you might as well quit crying. And while you're very appealing like that"—his eyes glazed with lust as he stared openly at her body from the doorway—"I have other plans for right now. I'll make us a couple of drinks while you slip into the lingerie I've left for you."

"Okay, Andrew." She let her voice quaver slightly. "Whatever you want."

"Oh, you'll be surprised at what I want," he promised with a frozen smile as he left the room. She heard the lock snap shut on the outside of the door.

Looking around the room, Emily could see no avenue of escape. She couldn't even signal out the window. And screaming would do her no good in a soundproof room on the fourteenth floor. She'd have to reach the main part of the apartment if she was going to come out of this alive. In the meantime, she'd play out his sick fantasy. Emily eyed the scrap of silk he expected her to wear.

And she'd have to find some clothes.

* * *

Mac ran flat out, all the way from the newspaper parking lot to the Masterbury Arms apartment building. He knew there was no way he could find Jack's car in the garage, but if he could get into the lobby, he'd be able to identify his employee's apartment from the building directory.

He was panting, as much from fear as from the two block sprint. His head swirled with the knowledge that he couldn't let Jack take Emily to his suite. If that happened, God only knew what the lunatic would do to her.

Mac skidded to a stop at the front door, expecting to find a doorman. There was no one. Suddenly, he saw movement in the back of the foyer near a bank of elevators. A woman stumbled out of an elevator cab, looked around wildly, then collapsed onto the floor.

It was Emily.

Mac's heart pounded at a ferocious rate. He ducked behind the edge of the door, careful to avoid being spotted. A man stepped out and yanked Emily to her feet. He glanced at his watch and around the foyer with a nod and a grin. Mac shook his head in frustration. Jack had obviously bribed the doorman to be away from the lobby so he could get Emily into the building.

Jack stepped back into the elevator cab, jerking Emily in behind him. Just as she was disappearing from sight, Mac moved forward and stood framed in the doorway. He prayed she'd seen him.

Desperate, he rattled the outside door, even as he knew it would be locked. Looking around, he spotted a cement ashtray. It was a few feet tall and filled with sand. Without a second thought, he picked it up, strode to the brass and beveled glass front doors of the Masterbury Arms deluxe apartment building and tossed the ashtray through the front door.

As Mac stepped over shattered glass, sand and cement, he reflected that the break in would prompt the doorman to summon the police. Whenever the man returned to his post, of course. Mac dropped one of his business cards on top of the mess. At least the doorman would know who was responsible for the damage.

He raced across the lobby to the elevators and watched as the one Emily was riding continued to climb. *What floor?*

It stopped at fourteen, hesitated for a short time, then began its return to the ground floor. The doors slid open to reveal an empty car.

Mac tore across the foyer to the directory. Damn, the list was alphabetical by tenant name. He searched for Jack Martin. It wasn't listed. The man had rented the apartment under an alias. Mac began again, looking beside every apartment listed on the fourteenth floor.

How am I going to figure this out in time? Even now, Emily was at that monster's mercy. He scanned the names frantically. There it was. Martin Jackson—apartment 1414.

I've got him.

Mac looked around the lobby, but couldn't spot a telephone. There was no time to search for a way to contact the police. He dashed back to the mess he'd made at the front door and scooped up his business card. He scribbled "Martin Jackson, apartment 1414" across the back and threw it back down where the doorman would find it.

Then, Mac stepped inside the elevator cab that had carried Emily and Jack to the fourteenth floor.

CHAPTER 17

Emily grabbed the bit of silk he expected her to wear and slipped it over her head. It fit her perfectly. He'd obviously remembered her very well from their first meeting at the newspaper and had purchased the chemise just for her.

She looked down at herself. The skirt barely skimmed the tops of her thighs, it was so short. And it was practically transparent. She pulled on the matching bed jacket. At least she was wearing something.

She slipped her feet into the stiletto-heeled mules in disgust. Not much for running, but she might as well leave them on, for now. Let Andrew think she was submissive. Besides, they might be a decent weapon.

Looking around the room again, she tried to decide where she should be when he returned. She didn't want to be sitting on the bed, as if she was waiting for him. If she positioned herself too near the door, it might appear as if she planned to ambush him.

Emily knew she'd have only one chance to escape.

After wandering to the video equipment, she pretended to study it. Soon, she heard the metallic click of a lock turning from the outside. He stood framed in the doorway.

"Checking it out?" His voice was too neutral.

"Well, I've never actually had video equipment in the bedroom."

"You'll like it," he growled low in his throat. "And it'll give me a souvenir."

Emily's heart thudded heavily in her chest, but she looked at him and smiled. "Something to remember me by?" Without giving him a chance to answer, she swayed towards him on the spike heels. She might as well take every advantage she could. She ran her hands down the front of the chemise. "How do I look?"

He stared at her, seemingly mesmerized. "Spectacular." It was barely more than a guttural grunt.

"Is that drink for me?" Emily reached out and stroked a fingernail lightly down the back of his hand.

"What?" He appeared to come out of a daze. "Yeah, one for each of us."

"You know what I want to do?" Her voice was a low-pitched purr and he leaned forward to hear her request. She took the wine glass from his hand and pressed the crystal against her bottom lip. She dipped the tip of her tongue into the chilled liquid. "I want to dance with you, Andrew. Nice and slow, with our bodies pressed together."

He stared at her, a frown creasing his brow.

"Won't you dance with me?" Emily pouted and tipped her head to one side. *Surely the beast knew how to dance.*

"Why do you want to dance?" Suspicion filled his face.

"I love dancing. I was going to suggest we go dancing on our second date. I think two people can get to know each other so much more intimately when they're slow dancing, don't you think so, too, Andrew? Would it be okay if we danced?" Emily asked his permission as she replayed Barbara's words about how this guy would demand control.

She wanted him interested and off guard. He had to think he was running the show. And she didn't dare provoke or confront him. That would definitely set him off and then, Emily had no doubt what the ending would be.

He looked at her a moment more as if assessing her offer. "I'd love to dance with you," he finally said.

"Do you have a CD player in here?" Emily pretended to look around even though she already knew there was no music source in the bedroom.

"No, but there's one in the living room. We'll be able to hear it in here."

"Great." He'd have to leave the door open as they danced, or the soundproofing would block out the music.

"What would you like to dance to?"

"You pick, lover." She set her wine glass on the bedside table.

He hesitated before he turned back to the living room.

Would he lock her in now? Possibly not, since he planned to return to the bedroom immediately after starting the music. She held her breath.

He paused with his hand on the door frame, then swung around and disappeared into the living room. If she stayed where she was, she might convince him she could be trusted, thereby getting him to drop his guard just a little more. That way, when an escape opportunity presented itself, she'd have a moment's head start.

Sounds of a romantic ballad drifted into the bedroom. Emily moved a scant few feet closer to the door, closed her eyes and swayed to the hypnotic beat. She knew how she must look, waiting for him in the bedroom, dancing alone. She felt his eyes on her when he returned.

Never letting on she was aware of him, Emily slid the bed jacket off her shoulders and hugged it to her body. Her head fall back as she shimmied in place.

She heard the ragged intake of his breath across the room, then the rush of his footsteps.

Suddenly, his hands were all over her as he growled hoarse obscenities that were barely intelligible. Emily swallowed hard to control the gagging his touch and words invoked. She fluttered her eyes and let her head tip back farther. Forcing herself to appear as if his touch ignited her, she sighed softly. "Mmm," she murmured, without opening her eyes. "Dance with me, Andrew. Please dance with me."

She folded herself against him, trapping his hands between their bodies, but he freed them and began stroking her intimately. Emily could sense his tenuous hold on his lust.

"Come on, baby," he whispered. "Closer."

He pulled her so tightly against him, she could feel his shirt buttons pressing into her. Emily leaned into him, humming and swaying to the soft sounds of the music, pulling him along with her. She tucked her head against his shoulder and slid her arms around his waist. Her skin crawled where he caressed her back.

His touch trailed onto her hips. She felt his fingers moving and realized he was lifting the hem of the chemise.

She clenched her teeth and cuddled closer against him just as his fingers brushed over the skin he'd bared. For a moment, he slid his hands over the firm globes of her buttocks, massaging her skin gently. Suddenly, he grabbed her roughly, tugging upwards, stretching her uncomfortably onto her toes. She tried to wiggle free, wondering what he wanted.

"Come on," he muttered harshly, "wrap your legs around my waist."

Emily let him lift her off the ground, then she bent her knees and folded her legs around him. Cradling her with one hand, he pushed her hair away from her face and gripped her face roughly with the other hand, pulling her mouth towards his. Just as his mouth was closing on hers, Emily writhed against him in simulated passion and he jerked back as if she'd bitten him. She arched her back and rolled her shoulders.

"Oh, Andrew," she moaned. "Why did you stop?" Without giving him an instant to answer, her fingers trailed down the line of buttons. "Why don't you let me make you more comfortable?" Her fingers worked the buttons, playing for time, trying to disorient him as she waited for the music to end.

He stood as if made of granite, staring at her as she slowly pushed his shirt off his shoulders.

"Wow." Emily ran her fingers over rock-hard pectorals and noted the ribbing on his abdomen where her legs bent around him. This guy was fit and strong. If she angered him, he would be physically capable of overwhelming and killing her. "I love a man who takes care of his body."

"You're no slouch yourself, Emma." His hands very nearly spanned her waist. He leaned forward and buried his face between her breasts. "I'm looking forward to being with you." His stubbled cheek rubbed roughly against the curve of her, abrading the soft skin.

Emily said nothing, just swayed to the beat of the music as he held her intimately against him. She could feel his arousal and sense his growing impatience. The music ended. Emily pouted and made herself rub the length of him as she slid down his body and took his hand. "I was just getting really into the mood, weren't you?"

"I'll put on another cd," he offered, turning toward the living room. She trailed along still holding his hand. He didn't seem to mind as she followed him out of the bedroom.

"What a great room," Emily gushed. She looked around with disguised horror at the animal heads mounted on every wall. "Did you shoot all these yourself?"

She saw his flush of pleasure and smiled to herself.

"Yes, I take a hunting vacation every year. The most exciting animal hunt I've ever been on was in Africa a couple of years ago." He gestured towards a gazelle head, its gentle expression frozen in death. "Both a lion and I were hunting her." He looked at Emily and smirked. "I won." He pointed to a framed photo on the mantel. Both the lion and the gazelle lay dead as he stood over them, his foot resting on the lion's neck.

"Wow. It must have been scary." She shivered prettily and looked around. "I love this fireplace. Can you turn it on?"

"Sure."

"We could turn off all the lamps, light some candles and dance in the firelight surrounded by your trophies. If you want to, that is."

He wavered for a moment, and she could tell he was nearly overcome by the headiness of her proposal. He studied her and she smiled at him as if enjoying an innocent game.

Emily turned. "I'll get the glasses if you want to grab the wine bottle from the fridge and put a couple of cd's in the player." She smiled playfully. "That way you're mine for the rest of the night. I can't wait to spread out on that zebra rug!"

As Emily hurried into the bedroom for the glasses, she prayed she'd convinced him to let her stay in the living room. As long as she remained out of the soundproofed bedroom, she stood a chance of making noise or escaping.

No footsteps trailed her. She scooped up the glasses and glanced down the hall. She could hear him in the kitchen. She had a moment.

The light switch was across the living room near the door. She raced to it. Pretending to be turning off the lights she examined the door. It was locked by a security system. She'd need the code to get it open "Damn," she swore softly under her breath.

He was coming back down the hall. She flicked off the light, meeting him in front of the couch.

"I've got the wine. Now, let me switch on the fireplace and we'll light some candles."

"You get the fireplace and pick the music. I'll light the candles," she offered.

He flipped a hidden switch and the gas fireplace roared to life. Flames fluttered eagerly over the ceramic logs. As he turned to play more music, Emily picked up a box of wooden matches and began lighting candles. There were several in the room and she wandered around, touching a flame to each wick. Carefully, she left an unlit match near several of the candles. She returned to the couch and tucked two matches between the cushions.

The music started as she settled onto the couch. He turned from the stereo and she smiled at him. He gasped for breath as she leaned forward to pick up his glass and refill it. Her breasts strained against the thin silk of the chemise, nearly overflowing the plunging neckline.

She leaned back, holding his glass to her lips, and crossed her legs for him. Running her bottom lip along the rim of his glass, she watched him.

"Come here," he rasped, holding out his hand. "I want you to dance."

She obediently rose and, slipping her feet back into the heels, walked across the room to him. She held out her arms and he shook his head roughly. "No, I don't want to dance with you. I want you to dance for me, Emma," he ground out roughly. "Show yourself to me."

"Really?" She pretended to be shy.

"Yes. I want to watch you." It was an order, not a request.

Emily let the music flow over her for a few moments. She closed her eyes and began to undulate in place. She watched him through slitted eyes. His mouth hung open, his eyes devoured her body. She expected him to begin drooling at any moment. She knew she didn't have long before he was on her, and prayed he dragged her to the couch or near one of the tables on which rested a candle. If he forced her down on the floor where they stood, she had nothing. She needed to be near a burning candle or matches.

Slowly, Emily began to move toward and away from her captor, never close enough for him to touch her or far enough so he thought she was leaving. She tempted him and withdrew, slowly making her way back to the area in front of the couch. He reached out for her and she let him touch her, not expecting the cruelty that stimulated him to complete arousal.

His fingers touched her through the silk, seizing her nipples, brutally twisting the flesh until she cried out in pain. He smiled in glee.

"That's my Emma," he crooned, his merciless eyes holding her in place. "Don't stop dancing for me." He wrenched again at her sensitive flesh. "Dance, Emma, dance just for me. I want to watch your body move just for me." She began to dance and he released his painful hold on her.

"Very good," he praised as he assessed her. "Now I want you to strip for me. And make it nice and slow." He sank onto the couch and picked up his wineglass.

Emily took a deep breath. She'd known it might come to this when she'd decided to stop this hunter in his tracks.

She still had every confidence she could end his reign of terror. He'd sadly underestimated her and she would have the last laugh when she took him down.

She pretended to be coy. "I've never done something like this before, Andrew."

He didn't say a word, just picked up her wineglass and tossed the contents over her. The silk clung to her. "I told you to get your clothes off. You can do it sexy for me or I can cut them off your body." Suddenly his knife was in his hand, firelight glinting along the length of blade as it sprung open.

His control was wavering.

"Okay, baby. Just let me get into it." She paused as if listening to the music, then began to sway. Slowly she pirouetted before him and let the bed jacket slip down her shoulders. She pulled it back up and then let it fall from one arm. Emily dragged it behind her as she wandered in a tiny circle and then put her spike-clad foot onto the table. She trailed the jacket the length of her leg and dropped it on the table beside her empty glass in a puddle of silk. She stepped back and out of the shoes.

"Put those back on," he ordered. "I like a woman in heels."

Without missing a beat, Emily slid her feet back into the mules and continued her dance, letting the straps of the chemise dangle down her arms. She was just trying to make up her mind whether to pull the garment over her head or slide it down when she heard a thumping sound.

He heard it, too, and turned abruptly toward the door.

"What the hell is that?" He muttered, rising abruptly to his feet.

She grabbed the jacket and slid it back on.

There was more noise and thudding sounds, then they could hear loud voices in the hallway. Suddenly, someone pounded at the front door.

"Comfort Gas. There's a gas leak in the basement. Anybody home?" The pounding continued.

Jack strode across the room and punched in the access code. Emily followed as closely as she dared and got every number. She smiled. He ripped open the door and glared up and down the hall. In every doorway, tenants stood in their night clothes, muttering and murmuring. The gas company representative was two doors down, his back to them, pounding on another door.

"Do you smell gas?" It was Jack's next door neighbor, sniffing at the air as if he could smell a basement gas leak on the fourteenth floor.

"No," he ground out. "I don't."

"The gas guy said we all had to get out."

* * *

"Right now?" Angered incredulity overwhelmed Jack. How could this be happening when he had everything planned? Now all these people would see Emma.

He paused. Then again, they wouldn't see her if he left her in the apartment. Jack swung back into his living room. No one had seen her yet. She was too shy to go into the hall wearing that skimpy outfit. He'd just lock her in and set the security code. If the whole floor was evacuated, no one would hear her, even if she yelled.

Once the all-clear was given, he'd take up where he'd left off. Jack smiled. She'd be even more at his mercy when she understood he had the power of life and death over her, leaving her in a building with a suspected gas leak. By the time he returned, she'd have lost any spunk she had left. This was working out very well.

"Guess we should go." Jack smiled at his neighbor who was already headed to the stairs. "But I'd better turn off my fireplace first."

Back in the apartment, he explained what was going on to Emily. "Of course, you'll have to wait here in the apartment. I don't want anyone to know you're…visiting me."

"You can't…just *leave* me here!" She seemed terrified.

"It's time you understand that you live"—he paused for effect—"*and die* by my choice, Emma. I'll expect you to finish what you've started for me when I return. Assuming there's been no explosion, of course."

She gasped. "Please, let me come with you."

"I said no. Do you want to sit in the living room or do I need to handcuff you to the bed in the other room?" He stared her down.

She hung her head. "Wherever you say."

"Fine, you can await your fate here in the living room. The phone has a lockout on it…so sorry, no phone calls to friends." He laughed at his own joke. "Finish off the bottle of wine if you want. I don't mind if you're drunk when I get back." He leered at her. "It might make you drop your inhibitions even more. And that might come in handy for you later when we get down to what I want from you."

* * *

Emily dropped heavily onto the couch, feigning submission. Inside, she was gleeful. Once he left, she'd contact headquarters and have him scooped up the moment his feet hit the sidewalk outside the building. Then, her joy faded.

She didn't have enough information to put him away for the series of rapes in Yorkton. She could file kidnap charges, but it would come down to a he said-she said scenario in court. He'd serve less time than he would if she got him on the multiple rape charge.

She had to make certain he paid for *all* his crimes. While he was gone, she'd have to search the apartment for any evidence she could find—gloves, ropes, ski masks—praying she found enough to make a case against him.

And she'd seize the opportunity to call for backup, too.

* * *

Keeping his back turned, Mac moved down the hallway away from Jack's apartment. When he heard the door slam and lock, he risked a glance. Jack was striding to the stairwell, obviously upset at the interruption of his evening.

The moment the door to the stairway closed on Jack's back, Mac flew to apartment 1414. He pounded on the door.

"Emily," he called, glancing toward the stairwell. "Emily, it's me. Open the door."

* * *

"Mac?" Emily flew to the door and punched in the code she'd seen Andrew use. "What are you doing here?"

"I saw Jack take you from your house. I followed the two of you here," he rasped pulling her into his arms and holding her against his chest. She felt the hard, rapid pounding of his heart under her cheek.

For a moment, Emily allowed herself to relax against Mac, basking in the safety. Then she pushed herself away from him.

"Jack? His name is Andrew Morrison."

"No. Jack Martin. You remember—he works in the personals at the *Daily Gazette*."

"He can't see you then, Mac. He'd recognize you. You've got to get out of here. And I have to find some evidence of his earlier rapes before they discover the source of the gas leak and the building is declared safe. Go on." Emily pushed and Mac didn't budge.

"No, Emily, you've got to leave now."

"Without evidence how can we put this guy away?"

"Emily," he looked at her, the love he felt for her evident in his eyes. "There *is no* gas leak. That story was the only thing I could think of to get Jack away from you before he attacked you. Please, come with me now."

"Mac," she reached up and stroked his cheek with her palm. "I can't leave without evidence. I am taking this guy down and I'm doing it tonight before he gets nervous and drops my alter ego, Emma. I can't let him get away with what he's been doing." Overflowing with her love for him, Emily dropped her hand and stepped away from Mac and back into the apartment. "I know you understand."

He looked down and she pushed the door to close it. Abruptly, the door stopped and she felt it opening again. Mac stepped through. "It'll go faster with two searching. We don't have long before he figures out it was a hoax. I just hope he doesn't realize someone is helping you."

With a brilliant smile, Emily locked the door and punched in the security code. "Let's get busy."

CHAPTER 18

Emily and Mac paused for a moment in the living room, glancing around. Where was the evidence? Barbara had guaranteed their hunter would need to keep his trophies close so he could look at them over and over again.

Emily pointed to a closed, swinging door. "That must be the kitchen." She nodded at another closed door. "Maybe that's an office. Why don't you start there. Wherever he's hidden the evidence, it's not going to be easy to find. He'll have a secret compartment or safe or drawer or something. You'll have to tear the place apart. I'll look in here."

She didn't say it, but they both knew Jack would expect to find her in the living room when he returned. Emily would be alone and the first to face his rage if he realized he'd been tricked.

With a nod, Mac headed for the closed door. It was locked and resisted his attempts to open it. It had been a long night and Mac appeared to have had enough of it. Emily watched as he stepped back and kicked the lock squarely with his heel. With a quick thunk of splintering wood, it gave way and the solid wood door fell open, revealing an office.

"Thank goodness, you didn't break the door," was all she said as he disappeared inside with a nod and a quick smile.

She looked at the door as Mac closed it behind him. As long as Jack didn't study it too closely, he shouldn't notice the damage. Just to be on the safe side, she turned off the lamp closest to the door so it would be shrouded in shadows.

Emily turned around and surveyed the living room. There didn't seem to be many places to hide things, but she peered behind the mounted heads on the wall. No hidden safes. She looked behind the compact discs and between the few books he had on the shelves. Nothing.

She heard Jack's key turn in the lock and barely had time to race back to the couch and throw herself on it. With a desperate quick look in the direction of the study, she grabbed her wine glass.

He slammed the door open so hard it banged against the wall. He strode through and crashed the door shut with a violence underlining his rage. Without turning around, he viciously punched in the alarm code. He stomped to the couch and stared down at her. Then he snatched his wineglass and drained it in a swallow. He refilled it and tossed down the second glass.

"Been enjoying yourself?" he growled.

"I was waiting for you."

"I was on a wild goose chase. It was some idiot's idea of a great prank."

"What happened?" Emily patted the couch beside her. It was like a surreal version of *Leave it to Beaver* with June Cleaver asking her husband how his day had been.

He threw himself on the sofa beside her. "When I got downstairs, along with a dozen other people from this floor, there was nothing going on—no police, fire, nothing. So, I asked about the gas leak." He sneered at her. "It was somebody's idea of a joke. Plus they were cleaning up a bunch of glass where some idiot had thrown the ash tray through the front door. What kind of society do we live in?"

If Emily hadn't been afraid for her life, she'd have laughed out loud. The man who had been terrorizing women in Yorkton, the one who planned to rape and kill her, was disturbed by what he perceived as poor behavior. Thankfully, he hadn't realized that behavior had been a ruse.

Emily prayed Mac was finding the evidence she'd need to put Andrew/Jack away forever. She looked up to see him staring at her.

"Were you scared, Emma?"

"Of course I was. I didn't know if the building was going to blow up or not. I didn't know if I was going to die right here."

He smiled as if he had a secret. "So, what did you do while you waited?"

"I looked out the window, I looked through the peephole into the hallway and I drank more wine." She held up her nearly empty glass and wiggled it. She pretended to contemplate. "There didn't seem to be much else to do since the door was locked." She hoped he'd think she was slightly tipsy from the wine.

His gaze chilled her to the marrow of her bones. "Well, now that I'm back, there's plenty to do. My little adventure downstairs has rejuvenated me."

Emily smiled at him. "Can I pour you more wine?" She leaned forward reaching for the bottle.

His hand closed around her forearm in a savage grip. "No more wine. I have other plans for us." He knocked her against the leather of the couch with a rough, backhanded shove.

Emily's head struck the wood frame and she fought for consciousness.

He stared at her, raking his eyes over her. Then he grabbed her by the arm and jerked her to him. Emily half slipped, half fell off the sofa and ended up on her knees in front of him.

"You will be on your knees eventually, but for now, get up." He kicked at her. "I want you to finish your dance for me, Emma."

She surged to her feet, determined to stay at arm's length from his punishing touch. Her glance flashed around and spotted the stereo. Looking back over her shoulder at him, she swayed across the room and started the music. She didn't care what was playing as long as she was far from his cruel hands.

The music flowed into the room and she began to wriggle in what she hoped was a sexy way. She raised her arms over her head and shimmied in place, swinging her hips to the music and watching Jack through half-closed eyes. She could tell he was excited by her actions. The evidence of his immediate arousal was easily seen. She leaned forward, affording him a tiny glimpse of her cleavage and straightened up again, swirling in a circle.

Emily watched him swallow deeply and pour himself more wine. He filled her glass as well. He settled back into the couch and sipped his wine as she continued to entertain him. The music slowed and drifted to an end and she paused with it, rotating her head to relax her neck muscles.

She heard his groan across the room.

"Come here," he ordered, reaching out. She knew pain awaited her.

The music resumed as Emily started toward him, so she pretended to be playful. She approached until she was just beyond his reach, then shuffled back, rolling her shoulders and batting her eyes at him. Jack seemed enthralled as he slumped on the couch, apparently mesmerized by her actions.

His eyes were glued to her breasts moving under the slithery silk chemise that occasionally afforded him a glimpse of her skin as she leaned forward. He bared his teeth in anticipation and Emily steeled herself. He was about to come at her, she knew. Suddenly, his head snapped to the right and he looked toward the darkened corner and his office door.

"Andrew," Emily's voice stroked at his name. "Why aren't you watching me?"

* * *

Jack turned back just as she twirled in a tight circle, allowing the chemise to float up around her. She moved quickly and he caught only a flash of ivory muscled buttocks and thighs. Then, she posed for him, and the silk fluttered back over her body, concealing her perfection from him again.

His delight in her game radiated through him as he stared at her standing sideways to him peering at him over her shoulder. He enjoyed watching her perform for him. Emma was as magnificent as he'd anticipated.

Jack felt blood thunder through his body, filling and engorging his manhood.

As the music crashed around them, he stared across the room to where Emily once again swayed and jiggled for his personal pleasure. He might as well take his time and enjoy everything she had to offer. After all, they had the whole weekend. And she was doing her best to please him.

Emily smiled at him and slid her tongue along her bottom lip. The whiplash of desire attacked him once more. Soon he would have to release himself with her.

* * *

Emily refused to look at the office door. She concentrated on distracting Jack and giving Mac time to search the office.

She redoubled her dancing efforts, allowing the sleeves of the bed jacket she wore to slide down her upper arms. She swayed close to the coffee table, staying away from Jack's reach. After grabbing her glass, she sipped the wine as she danced and circled in front of the man she knew planned to abuse and kill her.

The music ended. She turned back and smiled at the pervert who would be in custody shortly.

Jack was allowing his lust to show in his expression. "You're doing great, baby." His smile was terrifying. "The next song, you'll do more than dance, though. You'll strip just for me and then you'll be ready for me."

"But Andrew," Emily pouted. "I feel funny doing that. The dancing is kind of fun, but I don't know about stripping. I wasn't doing very well before you left."

"Trust me, you were doing fine. Besides, it's what I want, Emma-baby. And you're here to give me absolutely everything I want."

"Andrew," she began.

"There's no discussion." The music started again and he nodded at her. "Strip for me, Emma, and make it sexy. I want to see all of you, so don't hide anything. Your body was meant to be enjoyed by me in every way." He poured the last of the wine into his glass and leaned back into the tanned leather of the couch, smiling slightly. She knew he enjoyed watching her squirm.

Jack raised his glass in mock salute as the music swelled around them. "Get busy for me, baby."

Emily closed her eyes in mock surrender. If it would buy Mac more time, she'd have to do it. But she'd take her own sweet time. There was no way this man would see her naked.

She began to move to the music again, pulling the sheer bed jacket down her upper arms and back up, flipping up the hem of the skimpy nightgown she wore to offer glimpses of what her captor longed to see in full.

After a short time, she sensed his frustration peaking. Emily stepped onto the coffee table and wiggled her hips seductively in front of him as she allowed the jacket to slide down her arms and off. She waved it gently between them and dragged it over his head.

As she stepped off the table, she slipped it around his neck, pulling him to his feet. Her fingers flew over the buttons on his shirt without preamble, opening it. She pulled it from him and circled away, shirt dangling from her fingers. Emily let the straps of the chemise slip off her arms while she turned, smiling back at him and swaying enticingly.

With a lewd growl, Jack dropped heavily onto the couch, caressing the bed jacket that still curled around his neck. She knew he waited for her to turn and present him with her full glory.

Gritting her teeth in disgust, she slid her arms into his shirt and draped it around her. He was a bigger man than she'd realized, and for that, she was grateful. The shirt dangled almost to her knees, covering her well. Emily let the nightgown drift down under the shirt and onto the floor around her stiletto-clad feet.

With a glance from under her eyelashes, she stepped free of the silk and faced Jack, carefully remaining beyond his reach. Bending down she picked up the chemise and dangled it between them as she approached and dropped it onto his lap. Stepping back, she smiled and opened the shirt, just as she turned away from him, allowing him only a peek at her body. She heard his groan and felt his lust like a hot wind against her skin.

"Let me see you," he croaked.

"But you will," she promised, spinning once more as she opened the shirt and then pulled it around her, once more permitting him no more than a passing glance at her body. "I just want to tease you a bit. Isn't that how it's done?"

"Take off the shirt, Emma." His voice was a snarl and he began to rise to his feet.

She had to stay far enough away so he couldn't grab her. "Okay, Andrew, but don't rush me. I've never done this before and I'm kind of nervous. I mean I don't want to turn you off if I don't do it right." Her look begged his consent. "Please, let me do this the best I can for you."

He granted approval with a grunt. Slowly, she opened the neck of the shirt and looked at him before looking away shyly. She turned away from him and opened the shirt completely, allowing it to drop down revealing her back to him.

"Now turn around." His voice brooked no more delay.

Emily pulled the shirt back into place and turned to face him. His features froze into a mask of lechery, his sick hunger written all over it.

"Open the shirt."

Without a word, she let go of the front of the shirt. The curving orbs of her breasts peeked from between the fabric's edges but its draping folds still concealed her nipples. She could feel his eyes roam over her like cold, clammy hands and she fought to control her revulsion.

She prayed Mac would finish his search before she stood before this revolting man wearing nothing but ridiculous high heels. Emily waited for the final order to disrobe.

"Dance more, Emma-baby." The words were ground between clenched teeth.

Emily relaxed slightly. He wanted to lengthen his anticipation. Fine.

It gave Mac extra time in the office. She tilted her head and smiled at him.

"For you, Andrew," she murmured beginning to dance again.

She was careful to avoid excessive movement, granting him but glimpses of what he yearned to view. She watched him ogling her and she could tell a moment before he moved, that he'd observed her from a distance long enough.

He stood up and stretched, carefully placing his wine glass on the table.

"You've done great, Emma. You've got me in just the right mood." He started toward her, unbuttoning the top of his pants. "I think I'll first have you out here."

Emily stood still, willing herself not to run and not to attack him. He had to think her compliant and perhaps even frightened. Only then would he drop his guard. Above all, she couldn't permit him to take her into the soundproof room.

He crossed the room slowly and stopped in front of her. His hands didn't touch her flesh as he slipped the shirt off her shoulders, revealing her breasts. He sucked in his breath loudly and stared fixedly at her bared bosom, his hands still holding the shirt against her lowered forearms.

"They are spectacular. Are they real?" Now, even his words were meant to wound and degrade as he prepared to violate her.

"Of course they are." She pretended hurt outrage. "How dare you suggest otherwise?"

"I'm sorry, Emma, but so many aren't these days. Somehow, I knew yours would be real, though. And they're meant for my pleasure." He examined her critically. He ran an index finger across her abdomen. "You're even more beautiful than I anticipated. It's a shame I can't keep you indefinitely."

"Well, we're just getting to know one another. This could last quite a while, Andrew."

"I'm sorry, but what I have in mind isn't a long term relationship."

"I'm not interested in just a one-night stand, Andrew." She was careful not to challenge him directly. "You might find you'll want to spend a long time with me." She fed his fantasy. "I'm very good and I want to please you."

"Oh, Emma, we'll have the whole weekend together."

"But that—"

"That's all there'll be to it," he interrupted. "You seemed willing enough a minute ago."

"But I thought we were just starting something that would go on." Emily braced herself against the urge to close the shirt over her body.

"Well, you were wrong. I want you for the weekend. Maybe a couple more days if you're as good as your dance suggests. But then it's over." His voice left no doubt he'd end her life at his discretion.

Emily turned away, pulling the shirt around her. If she looked into those cruel, unfeeling eyes for a moment longer, she wouldn't be able to keep up the act. She pretended to cry, heaving her shoulders in silent, imaginary sobs. "I thought you really liked me, Andrew. I thought tonight was some kind of a game."

"It's a game all right. But it's not exactly the one you think."

Emily felt his open hand touch her shoulder blade and she shivered. She hoped he thought it was fear or passion and not anger that rocked her to her core.

Whether Mac had found the evidence or not, she was going to take action. This creature would never hunt or abuse again. The game he sought to play to its grisly end would have a very different outcome than he planned.

As his fingers crawled over her shoulder like a wandering spider, she braced herself. He stepped closer and she took a deep breath.

"It's over." The deep voice did not shout, but the words rocked the room.

Jack and Emily spun around. Backlit, Mac stood framed in the doorway to the office, his face in shadow, holding Jack's scrapbook in his hand. He gestured with it. "Your sick hunting contest is over, Jack, and you're going away for a long time."

"What the hell are you doing in here? Get out and leave that behind."

"I'm not going anywhere."

"Then you die, too." Jack swung back to face Emily. "But not until this one gets what she deserves." He raised his arm, fist clenched.

In one fluid movement, Emily drove her knee into his groin with every ounce of energy she possessed. With an explosive gasp, air bursting from his lungs, Jack dropped to his knees in front of her. Like lightning she struck again, her knee crashing into his chin. His eyes rolled into his head as he collapsed on the floor, unconscious.

Emily smiled at Mac as they stood over the fallen body of Jack Martin, the man whose career in terror they'd just ended. "Do you want to call 911, or shall I?"

Mac dropped the grisly trophy album onto the coffee table and scooped her into his arms. Resting his chin on the top of her head, he held her close.

"I was so afraid for you," he murmured, stroking her back with tender hands. "I thought I'd never find the evidence in time. Then I'd have to confront him to help you, and he'd walk away from this."

She tipped back her head, her green eyes sparkling. "We make quite a team, Mr. Managing Editor."

Just then a loud crash shattered the silence and the front door. A battering ram had made short work of Jack's security system. A team of police stood framed in the doorway, Ryan and Angela in front. Their service revolvers drawn, the officers scanned the scene, then visibly relaxed.

"Got everything under control I see, Em." Angela's worry was wiped away by a broad smile blooming across her face.

"I think someone else will have to read this scum bag his rights," said Ryan. "When he comes to, that is." He struggled to keep a straight face.

Emily snagged the album off the table. "Nice of him to collect the evidence for us. Looks like we got him. He's going to prison for a very long time."

"That's not all," said Angela. "The team sent to your house found blood droplets on the pocket of your purse and the kitchen wall. I'm sure it'll match the DNA sample we have from one of his earlier attacks."

Mac and Emily smiled into each other's eyes. "We did it," she whispered.

"You better believe it."

EPILOGUE

"So, what do you think of your perfect designer house now?" Emily asked with a smile as the Keeshond puppy bounded across the ceramic tiles in the kitchen and slid to a halt in front of the water bowl. He reached out a paw and splashed in the dish.

Mac walked toward Emily, a smile on his face. Morning sunshine sparkled through the kitchen as he slid his arms around her from behind and caressed her swollen belly. "In a few months, it'll be *more* than the perfect home."

He sighed in contentment as his wife spun around in his embrace and pressed her lips to his. He responded to her kiss, gliding his hands over her back and down onto her hips. He gently tugged her more intimately to him.

"I love you, Mac," Emily said with a contented sigh. "I love you so much."

"I love you, too, Emily. Whatever did I do before you came into my life?"

"Well, I'd have to say you just existed." Emily couldn't help teasing him, then confessed, "Just like I did."

"Thank you for saving me, my darling."

"You're more than welcome, Mac, but it seems to me we saved each other."

"*And*, between the two of us, made certain Jack Martin will be locked away for the rest of his unnatural life," Mac said with pride.

"I never doubted we would."

"You had me pretty scared back then."

"Don't forget that I was scared, too. But it's all over now." Emily smiled at her husband, feeling pure joy radiate through her. "We're together forever."

"Forever," he agreed.

LIBBY MCKINMER

Words have formed the cornerstone of Libby's life. Her father read poetry to Libb's mother during her pregnancy…and the love of reading and writing was born with her. She was a "library brat" as a child, visiting regularly to feed her desire to read.

Libby concentrated on a Bachelor's Degree in English Literature and Classical Literature and was the first to graduate from her university with a double major in this combination.

This writer has always been a voracious reader, too, and usually has several books on the go at any given time. Mystery, romantic-suspense, spy thriller or mainstream—if it's well-written and engaging, she enjoys it.

Libby has been the creative director of a radio station, a newspaper reporter and editor, the editor of one national and several corporate newsletters, and the senior editorial director of a regional women's magazine. Additionally, she has written dozens of freelance magazine articles from an interview with an Olympian to "How-To" articles.

In addition to writing, Libby is also an editor and has worked with many authors on award-winning books. "I love taking a good book and helping an author make it the best it can be. And if she or he wins an award with that book, I'm so proud!"

Outside of her professional life, Libby has always enjoyed having a variety of animals in her life. You'll notice most of her central characters have pets. "Main characters just aren't complete if there isn't a cat, dog, bird or some other pet in their lives. It helps me see what that character is like as a person," said Libby with a grin, surrounded by her furry writing partners.

Libby was a member of the Delta Society and developed one of the first pet-facilitated therapy programs in her community.

If you'd like to write to her, please feel free to do so at libbymckinmer@libbymckinmer.com. She's always thrilled to hear from her fans.